Dear I

I love writing ... saying
... when my editor
... pleased to introduce the
... Madison and Katrina, who enjoy life and love
... on Victoria Hospital.

What drew me to their stories? Several things. Firstly, I wanted to set myself a challenge and do something a little bit different—so the stories actually take place in more or less the same timeframe. This meant I had to keep the events of Madison's story very much in mind when I wrote Katrina's! (THE CHILDREN'S DOCTOR'S SPECIAL PROPOSAL is available next month). Secondly, I was thinking about fairy tales and Prince Charming: in modern days, do you have to go and look for your prince, or will he come and find you? Add the fact that there's something irresistible about a Mediterranean doctor and even more so about ruined castles (I spent a week in Wales during the summer while I was planning the books and fell in love with the area—not to mention the recipe in Katrina's story, which my editor begged for before I'd even written the book!). And, finally, the books have a lot of me in them: Madison shares my love of music and Katrina, like me, has impaired hearing.

And the little country church at the very end of Katrina's story? Actually, that's real (albeit moved to suit my fictional world). I was privileged to attend a special family wedding there just as I was writing the wedding scene—which is why I've dedicated the second story to my cousin Lee and his lovely bride Lucy, and also borrowed the weather from their day…

So with this in mind I had a lot of fun creating Madison and Katrina's world. I hope you enjoy reading their stories as much as I enjoyed writing them.

I'm always delighted to hear from readers, so do come and visit me at www.katehardy.com

With love

Kate Hardy

Kate Hardy lives in Norwich, in the east of England, with her husband, two young children, one bouncy spaniel, and too many books to count! When she's not busy writing romance or researching local history, she helps out at her children's schools. She also loves cooking—spot the recipes sneaked into her books! (They're also on her website, along with extracts and stories behind the books.) Writing for Mills & Boon has been a dream come true for Kate—something she wanted to do ever since she was twelve. She's been writing Medical™ Romances for nearly five years now, and also writes for Modern Heat™. She says it's the best of both worlds, because she gets to learn lots of new things when she's researching the background to a book: add a touch of passion, drama and danger, a new gorgeous hero every time, and it's the perfect job!

Kate Hardy is the winner of the RNA Romance Prize 2008 for her Modern Heat™ novel BREAKFAST AT GIOVANNI'S.

Kate's always delighted to hear from readers, so do drop in to her website at www.katehardy.com

---

Recent titles by the same author:

Medical™ Romance
THE SPANISH DOCTOR'S LOVE-CHILD
THE DOCTORS ROYAL LOVE-CHILD
(Brides of Penhally Bay)
THE ITALIAN GP'S BRIDE

Modern Heat™
HOTLY BEDDED, CONVENIENTLY WEDDED
SOLD TO THE HIGHEST BIDDER!
BREAKFAST AT GIOVANNI'S

THE GREEK DOCTOR'S NEW-YEAR BABY

BY

KATE HARDY

First published in Great Britain 2008
Paperback edition 2009
Harlequin Mills & Boon Limited,
Eton House, 18-24 Paradise Road, Richmond, Surrey TW9 1SR

ISBN: 978 0 263 86817 3

Set in Times Roman 10½ on 12¼ pt
03-0109-51045

Printed and bound in Spain
by Litografia Rosés, S.A., Barcelona

What people are saying about Kate Hardy…

'THE ITALIAN GP'S BRIDE is a spellbinding romance that I devoured in a single sitting! Kate Hardy is a fabulously talented writer whose books never fail to make me laugh, cry and care, and THE ITALIAN GP'S BRIDE is the latest in a long line of captivating romances that have made her one of my all-time favourite writers.'
—Cataromance on THE ITALIAN GP'S BRIDE, Medical™ Romance August 07

Look out for Kate Hardy in Modern Heat™!

'BREAKFAST AT GIOVANNI'S is simply terrific! Sexy, funny, tender, passionate and romantic, this engrossing tale features a loveable heroine and a gorgeous Italian hero who will make you swoon! Kate Hardy is a writer readers can count on in order to deliver an entertaining page-turner which they will devour in a single sitting, and BREAKFAST AT GIOVANNI'S is certainly no exception. So take the phone off the hook, put your feet up and lose yourself…'
—Cataromance on BREAKFAST AT GIOVANNI'S, July 07

For Annette, Grant, Amy and Lauren,
With love.

CHAPTER ONE

MADISON noticed him the moment he walked into the room.

Despite the fact that the hospital's charity ball was heaving with people, all wearing Venetian masks—and he was dressed the same as all the other men in a dinner jacket, dark trousers, white shirt and bow-tie, plus a plain gold eye mask—there was something about the tall, dark-haired man that set him apart from the others. Some kind of energy that drew her eye.

Not that she was going to do anything about it. Not tonight.

As the chair of the committee for the hospital's fundraiser ball, Madison Gregory had work to do. Such as making sure that everything was running like clockwork behind the scenes. Being there to troubleshoot any last-minute problems. Charming people with a sweet smile and fixing any little niggles without a fuss.

But so far any problems had been minor, because everything had been planned down to the last detail. There had been a few murmurs at first in committee meetings when she'd suggested a jazz trio—a band she'd heard several times at her favourite club—but Madison had stuck to her guns. In her view, a rock band really didn't suit a masked ball, and although ballroom dancing had become popular again, thanks to TV shows, having a string quartet playing waltzes would have felt too formal. Whereas soft, easy-listening jazz—bright upbeat numbers and slow crooning ballads that people knew and could dance to—was perfect for a ball.

Now she could even see couples mouthing the words of 'Fly Me to the Moon' to each other, smiling and laughing and just having fun on the dance floor. Relief flooded through her. She'd got it right. This was going to work.

With this lovely, warm, relaxed atmosphere, people would be more willing to be parted from their money. They'd buy loads of tickets for the tombola prizes she and the rest of the committee had talked local companies into donating—balloon rides, spa treatments and a chocolate hamper that her cousin and best friend Katrina desperately wanted to win and had bought so many tickets in lieu of being at the ball that Madison had decided, if Katrina didn't win it, she'd buy her the very same hamper as consolation.

And maybe, just maybe, the fund for the new scanner would reach the halfway point as a result.

Eve, one of the senior nurses from the emergency department, came up to her. 'Maddie, you've been rushing around since an hour before everything started. Why don't you take a break?'

A little voice in Madison's head added, *And go and find out who the man in the gold eye mask is.* She brushed it aside and smiled at Eve. 'It's OK. I'm fine.'

'You paid for a ticket, too,' Eve reminded her. 'Which means you're entitled to dance and have some fun. Just because you're the chair of the organising committee, it doesn't mean you can't enjoy yourself.'

'I *am* enjoying myself.' And it was true: Madison loved being in the thick of things. She'd been hard put to choose between specialising in emergency medicine and her final choice, obstetrics, because she enjoyed the buzz of being too busy almost as much as she loved those magical first minutes of a new life.

And then, as the music changed and the pianist seemed to flow seamlessly into 'It Had to be You', a hand touched her arm.

'May I?' a deep, unfamiliar and slightly accented voice asked.

Even before she looked up, she knew who it was going to be, and a shiver ran down her spine.

The man in the gold mask.

He was looking at her with the most sensual, smouldering gaze she'd ever seen: dark eyes with a hint of green and gold and grey. Stunning.

Not to mention a slow, sweet smile that actually made her knees go weak.

'I...' Her throat dried, and Eve gave her a shove.

'She means yes,' Eve said sweetly. 'Have fun.'

Before Madison could protest, she was dancing with the stranger.

Theo had been aware of her all evening: the girl in the floaty dress with the pink and gold cat mask covering her upper face and the most incredible smile. He'd seen her talking and laughing with plenty of people, though he hadn't actually seen her on the dance floor.

And now he was dancing cheek to cheek with her. Whoever had chosen this music was an utter genius: it had neither the formality of ballroom dancing nor the slight distance of pop. This was old-fashioned dance music, the kind of stuff his grandparents loved—and, so he'd discovered recently, his mother had loved too.

Despite his dance partner's high-heeled shoes, she wasn't that tall and he had to dip his head slightly to dance with her, but she felt perfect in his arms. And those blue, blue eyes behind the mask were just stunning. Like a Mediterranean sky on a late summer evening, shading to dark navy at the very edges of her irises. Her dark hair was loose around her shoulders—not perfectly straight, but not a riot of curls either. Soft, enticing waves that made him want to tangle his hands in them, feel the silkiness against his fingertips.

Even more than that, he wanted to see her hair spread over his pillow. And he really, really wanted to explore that beautiful mouth. Tease it with kisses until it opened beneath his mouth, letting him deepen the kiss.

Kyrios. He couldn't remember when he'd last felt a pull of attraction this strong.

But right now she was in his arms, holding him close. And it felt good.

The stranger's touch was perfectly decorous, Madison thought. And yet somehow it felt personal—intimate, even. They were dancing close enough for her to feel his breathing, hear his heartbeat. And he had a perfect sense of rhythm, guiding her round the floor so effortlessly that it actually felt like floating. She'd never been so in tune with a dance partner before.

They didn't speak as they danced—they didn't need to—and suddenly everyone around them just melted away. They could have been dancing on a little terrace overlooking a garden in Tuscany, just the two of them, in the moonlight…

She shook herself. Of course not. This was *London*. And if it wasn't for the fact that she'd deliberately stuck to sparkling water because she was responsible for the way things ran tonight, she would've been sure this heady feeling was from drinking too much champagne—almost like tiny bubbles fizzing through her veins.

The fact it was all from dancing with him scared her and excited her at the same time. She'd never reacted this strongly to anyone before. Even Harry.

Part of her wanted to ask the stranger what his name was, but she knew that talking would break the spell. And right now she didn't want it to end. Just the two of them and the music, the singer crooning and the soft jazzy piano counterpointed by the double bass and guitar.

Two and a half minutes had never passed so slowly.

Or so very, very fast.

When the song ended and his hands dropped from her body and he took a step backwards, it felt so wrong.

And then he bowed to her, lifted her right hand and kissed the pulse on the inside of her wrist.

She could barely breathe.

His eyes—dark and as sexy as hell—held hers. 'Thank you.'

Again, that slight accent. She couldn't quite place it, but it was incredibly attractive.

Just as her mouth started to frame a response, an introduction, a question, a different pair of arms caught her round the waist. 'Maddie! Here's my girl.' She found herself spun into a hug. Into arms she recognised—Ed, the registrar in the emergency department she'd dated a couple of times, a month or so back.

Oh, help.

Ed was beaming. A champagne-induced sort of beaming, and he'd clearly forgotten that they'd agreed to be just good friends—that they weren't dating any more.

By the time Madison had extricated herself and jollied Ed into remembering that they were just friends and she was busy tonight anyway with her chairwoman hat on, and had informed him that he'd just been incredibly rude to the man who'd danced with her by cutting in like that, Mr Gold Mask was nowhere to be seen.

The disappointment felt as if someone had just driven past her through a deep puddle, dousing her in cold water.

Which was utterly ridiculous. The man was a complete stranger. No way should she be reacting this strongly to him—

a man who'd danced with her once and whom she was unlikely to see again, because she certainly didn't recognise him as one of the hospital staff she'd chivvied into getting a table together.

Madison Gregory, you need to get a grip, she told herself silently, then went to check that everything was proceeding smoothly with the tombola.

Here's my girl.

Well, of course a woman that attractive wouldn't be single. Even though Theo had instinctively checked her left hand before asking her to dance and there had been no sign of a ring, he should've realised that she would have a boyfriend.

And a dance was just a dance. It wasn't going to lead to anything else.

He pushed away the regret. It wasn't as if he was looking for a relationship anyway. Wasn't that half the reason why he'd left Greece, because his family was constantly trying to fix him up with an eligible woman and it was driving him crazy? And he was only here tonight because he was at a loose end the weekend before he started his new job. Buying a ticket for the hospital fundraiser had seemed like a good idea—a chance to meet some of his new colleagues socially, get to know people. He'd enjoyed chatting to people tonight.

But all the same he needed some fresh air. A cool breeze to bring his common sense back and give him some immunity to the sweet, seductive tones of the singer. As she segued into 'Bewitched, Bothered and Bewildered', he allowed himself the briefest of smiles. Theo Petrakis most definitely didn't let himself get bewitched, bothered and bewildered by anyone.

And that included a beautiful—and very much off-limits—woman by the name of Maddie. He'd go back in, buy a few tombola tickets to help swell the fundraising coffers…and then maybe he'd have an early night.

Madison kept the smile on her face for the rest of the evening. And although she allowed herself to relax in between checking that all was well and danced with a dozen different men, none of her partners on the dance floor matched up to the man in the gold mask. They didn't have his fluidity or his intuitiveness.

It was pretty stupid even to be thinking about the man. She'd never met him before—or she would most definitely have remembered—and she probably wouldn't meet him again.

She didn't even know his name.

And you couldn't fall for someone whose name you didn't even know…could you?

She shoved the thought to the back of her mind. Besides, tonight wasn't about her. It was about raising money for the new and hugely expensive medical equipment that the hospital trust dearly wanted but just couldn't afford. So she was going to schmooze and schmooze and talk people into buying more tombola tickets.

When the evening was over and everyone had gone home, Madison stopped by the hotel kitchens to thank the staff for their hard work and deliver the chocolates she'd bought them to show her appreciation, then headed for the hospital. Right now, she was wide awake—and unless Katrina, as the on-call doctor, was in with a patient, the chances were she'd be free for a quick coffee-break.

When the night sister let her into the paediatric department, Madison was delighted to discover that her cousin was in her office, catching up with paperwork.

'You missed a great evening,' she said, settling herself on the edge of Katrina's desk. Even though Katrina, being deaf, wasn't over-keen on dark, noisy, crowded environments, Madison knew that her cousin would have enjoyed the ball.

'I wanted to be there, Maddie, you know that—but we're so short-staffed right now I just couldn't work it.' She looked hopefully at Madison. 'So, did you take my hamper back to your place before dropping in? Or have you scoffed half of it already?'

Madison shook her head. 'Sorry, hon. You didn't win it. But you did get a full body massage and a manicure.' She produced the vouchers from her handbag.

Katrina smiled wryly. 'Can you see *me* having a manicure?'

'Well—no,' Madison admitted. She enjoyed doing girly things, but her cousin most definitely didn't. Katrina was practical. Too practical for her own good.

'Then *you* have them. With my love.'

Madison shook her head. 'I can't do that. You spent a fortune on tickets, Kat.' And she hadn't won a single thing—so Madison had told a teensy fib and given her cousin her own prizes. 'Look, at least have the massage. You'd enjoy it. Really, you would. It's really relaxing.'

Katrina wrinkled her nose. 'Thanks, but it's not my style.' And she clearly suspected Madison of having had a hand in the prizes—which she had, but not quite in the way Katrina thought. 'Look, if you really don't want them, I'll raffle them off in the department and you can add the proceeds to the scanner fund.' Katrina paused. 'Did you meet Prince Charming tonight, then?'

'Hey, are you calling me Cinderella?' Madison teased.

'You've gone red. Aha. So you *did* meet someone.' Katrina gave her a wicked smile. 'Come on. Details. All of them. Right now.'

Madison shrugged. 'There's not a lot to tell. We danced. Once.' She left out the fact that the man in the gold mask had kissed her inner wrist and she could still feel the touch of his mouth against her skin.

'And?' When Madison didn't reply, Katrina asked, 'What's his name? Which ward is he on?'

'No idea, to both.' Madison forced herself to sound offhand. 'Kat, it was just a dance.' *And a kiss.* 'And he was wearing a mask, so I didn't even get to see his face.'

But she had seen his eyes and his mouth. She'd class both as the sexiest she'd ever seen.

'You didn't even ask? Sounds like you missed a great opportunity,' Katrina said. 'He might have been really nice.' She shook her head. 'You're so picky. How are you ever going to meet someone if you never give them a chance?'

Madison grinned. 'Says the woman who's waiting for her prince to come and find her.'

'I looked. I kissed some of them, even. And they turned into frogs.' Katrina shrugged. 'Anyway. I'm happy with my career.'

'So am I,' Madison said.

Katrina raised an eyebrow. 'Honey, you've been broody for the last five years.'

'Which is why I made such a huge mistake with Harry. I know.' Madison shrugged. 'Next time, I'll get it right. Find myself the perfect man—gorgeous body, gorgeous mind, gorgeous heart.'

'In that order?'

'Colour me shallow.' Madison laughed and spread her hands. 'Actually, the order doesn't matter, as long as they're all present.' Though she knew which ones were the most important. The two Harry had turned out not to possess.

'I think you're going to have to compromise somewhere,' Katrina said.

Madison shook her head. 'No compromising.' Not any more. She'd compromised with Harry, and look where that had got her. Divorced and disillusioned at the age of twenty-six. Except now, at thirty, she had her bounce back again. 'Look, our mums managed it, didn't they?'

'I'm not so sure our dads are perfect,' Katrina said thoughtfully. 'I love Dad and Uncle Bryan to bits, but they're not perfect, Maddie. Nobody is. They're only human.'

Madison was saved from having to agree by a soft knock on the door. 'Kat, sorry to interrupt—I need you to come and have a look at Joseph. I'm not happy with his obs,' the paediatric nurse said, looking worried.

'On my way,' Katrina said. 'Sorry, Maddie.'

'Hey. I only dropped in to give you your prizes. I'll catch you later.' Madison hugged her cousin, and left the ward.

But she still couldn't get that kiss out of her head. It had been chaste and decorous—yet, at the same time, the hottest thing she'd ever experienced. Full of promise. If Ed hadn't interrupted, who knew what could have happened?

'Get a grip, Maddie. Real world,' she informed herself. The ball was over. And she'd probably never see the stranger again, so what was the point in wondering what might have been?

CHAPTER TWO

ON MONDAY morning—the day before he was supposed to start—Theo Petrakis walked on to the maternity unit.

He liked what he saw. Everything was organised—well, as organised as you could get in a ward where babies decided to arrive earlier than expected, or made their parents wait around and worry before they finally made their appearance—and there were plenty of hand sanitation gel dispensers around, so clearly they were hot on hygiene here. And the warm, relaxed atmosphere he'd noticed at his interview was still present, to his relief. Before now he'd worked in a unit where the midwives and doctors had been practically ranged against each other instead of recognising that they were a team.

'Can I help you?' the midwife sitting at the reception desk asked.

He smiled at her and held out his hand. 'I'm Theo Petrakis. Strictly speaking, I'm not supposed to be here until tomorrow, but I thought I'd drop in and say hello.'

'Theo Petrakis—our new consultant, yes?' She returned the smile. 'I'm Iris Rutherford.' The senior midwife, according to her name badge. She took his hand and shook it warmly. 'Pleased to meet you. Especially as you've picked a nice quiet moment.'

'As opposed to three in the morning, when all the babies decide it's the perfect time to make their arrival?' he asked wryly.

She laughed. 'Too right! If you've got a few minutes spare, I can show you around and introduce you to everyone.'

'Thanks. I'd like that.'

And by everyone, Theo discovered, she *meant* everyone, including the health-care assistants.

It had definitely been a good decision to take this temporary post, he thought. A six-month stint as a locum for the senior consultant, who was off on long-term sick leave. It would broaden his experience so he was ready to make the step up to a senior consultancy role. As it looked as if he'd be part of a team here that believed in working together, this job was going to be a real pleasure.

Then he noticed the slight frown on Iris's face as they got back to her desk. 'What's up?'

'I was hoping you'd get to meet our registrar, but she's in one of the delivery rooms right now. She's brilliant at her job, good with the mums and the babies. She's going to make an excellent consultant in a couple of years.'

'Ambitious?' Theo asked, trying to read between the lines.

Iris smiled. 'She certainly hasn't met the man who'll come between her and her career. But she won't give you a hard time for taking over from Doug, if that's what you're asking.'

By the time Theo left the ward, the registrar still hadn't emerged from the delivery room—and no way would he interrupt what was clearly already a difficult situation for a woman in labour—but he wasn't particularly worried about not meeting her before he started. If she was anything like her colleagues, they'd get along just fine.

The following morning, again the registrar wasn't there when he arrived because she was helping out with a difficult birth. But he was just making himself a mug of coffee when she walked into the ward's kitchen.

'Hello. You must be the new…' She stopped dead, clearly recognising him.

Just as he recognised her.

Even without the mask, he knew her instantly. Those beautiful eyes. That mouth. The prickle of awareness that ran all the way down his spine.

Which was crazy.

Apart from the fact he never mixed work and relationships, it would be impossible here anyway. He was only here for six months, and she was involved. The best he could hope for was a good working relationship. Which meant defusing any embarrassment right from the start.

'Doctor,' he finished lightly. 'Yes. I didn't get a chance to introduce myself to you at the ball on Saturday. Theo Petrakis.' He held out his hand.

'Madison Gregory. Everyone calls me Maddie. Welcome to the ward.' She took his hand.

Using her right hand. And he'd kissed her right wrist on Saturday night, touched his lips to the pulse point.

The impulse to do it again shocked him, it was so strong. He just about managed to shake her hand and then drop it again. 'I was making coffee. The kettle's hot. What can I get you?'

'I'm impressed. You're well trained,' she teased.

He shrugged. 'I don't mind taking my turn to make coffee. I certainly don't intend to pull rank and expect my team to run around after me.'

'Doug'll be pleased to know his department's in safe hands—and that you share his attitude towards the team,' she said. 'Thanks. That'll be a lot of milk and no sugar for me, please. And a little bit of cold water, too, so it's cool enough to drink.'

A trick most doctors learned very early on, Theo knew. If

you waited for your drink to cool, the chances were you wouldn't even get a first sip before you were called to a patient. 'Busy morning, hmm?' he asked.

She nodded. 'But I love mornings like this. When things look as if they're going to go pear-shaped, and all the worst-case scenarios are running through your head while you're maintaining absolute calm to stop the mum and her partner worrying—and then suddenly it all works and you end up with a new mum and dad, all misty-eyed and cuddling their little miracle. That first moment when the whole world seems brand new.'

Clearly she loved her job. And he knew what she meant: those first moments with a newborn baby always took his breath away, too.

He made the coffee the way she'd specified and handed the mug to her.

'Thanks.' She took a sip. 'Oh-h-h. This is perfect. Just what I needed.'

She seemed to be about to say something else, but then her pager bleeped. She glanced at the readout, then sighed and put the mug on the draining board. 'Sorry. I'll finish it later. I have to go. The emergency department needs a second opinion on a pregnant patient with back pain.'

'Can I come and observe?' he asked.

She blinked, looking faintly surprised. 'Well, if you really want to, sure. I'm not worried about someone senior observing me,' she added, 'but four would definitely be a crowd and I had intended to take my fourth-year students down with me.'

'Your students?'

His surprise must have sounded in his voice because she admitted, 'Strictly speaking, I suppose they're *your* students, but before Doug went on sick leave he agreed I could take over the mentoring side of things. And Sanjay and Nita are doing really well—especially Sanjay, who's blossomed since he's been with us. I want to keep his confidence up.'

Theo raised an eyebrow. 'I thought only consultants were mentors.' And she was a registrar, wasn't she?

'Look, I'll explain on the way down to ED. If you want to observe, we'd better not take the students with us this time—it's not fair to our mum to have too many people in a cubicle with her, especially as she's in the emergency department and probably panicking like anything right now. Plus Sanjay and Nita really need to meet you properly before you observe them.'

Theo had to suppress a smile at the way Madison was taking control when officially she was his junior, but he liked her confidence and the way her first thoughts were for other people's well-being. 'Sure.'

She stopped off at the reception desk and rang down to the emergency department to reassure them that she was on her way, then ushered him out of the department.

'So talk me through the mentoring stuff,' he said.

'You know as well as I do, we have a recruitment crisis in our specialty,' she said. 'All the surveys say that students don't want to work in obs and gynae because they have such a bad time on rotation—either they're made to feel they get under the feet of the midwives, or they're stuck in the furthest corner of an operating theatre watching a Caesarean.'

'So they never really get to do any of the work and they don't feel part of the team.'

'Exactly,' Madison said. 'We're organised nowadays so the team means a whole department, rather than the old way of having a "firm" of a consultant, registrar and house officers who always work together, and in a way that's a shame because it makes it harder for junior doctors to settle into the team. I really think students need a single point of contact in a department to help them feel they're really part of what's going on. Yes, they have to sort out their logbooks and what have you, but they also need proper contact with patients and they need *real* jobs to do if they're to get the best out of their attachment.'

'Responsibilities for something practical, such as a departmental audit,' Theo suggested.

That earned him another of the gorgeous smiles. 'Absolutely. On our ward, we have two students at a time on attachment. I'm responsible for bedside teaching, and they attend my clinic and theatre sessions.'

'Are you pure obstetrics?' Theo asked.

She nodded. 'Though I'm interested in foetal medicine as well.'

'So what about the gynae work?'

'I liaise with the consultants and the other registrars so the students get sessions with them, too—but I'm still their point of contact if they're worried about anything, or if they want to see more of a particular subspecialty outside pure obstetrics. I also get them to spend time with the midwives, so they develop a rapport and a bit of respect for our colleagues, as well as a chance to see some low-risk births.'

'Instead of thinking that life in our ward is all epidurals and emergency sections,' Theo agreed. 'That sounds good. I notice you have a sensory room here.'

'And a water-birth suite. We want our mums to have the best, most natural and relaxing experience possible. Our midwives are fantastic, and we only intervene when we're asked for help.'

'Amen to that,' he said feelingly.

The emergency registrar met them practically at the door and gave them a swift handover. Theo recognised the man's voice—he was the one who'd swept Madison off her feet at the ball. Yet Madison didn't greet him as if there was anything more than a professional relationship between them. And Iris had said that Madison hadn't met the man to come between her and her career. So did that mean she was single after all?

Crazy. He shouldn't even be thinking about her like that.

And yet he couldn't take his eyes off her. There was something about her. Something that made him want to break all his personal rules.

Which was even crazier.

The registrar introduced them both to the patient, then left to see the next on his list.

'Mrs Ellis, I'm Madison Gregory and this is Theo Petrakis,' Madison said. 'Ed called us from the maternity department. I understand you've been having back pain.'

Mrs Ellis nodded. 'And it hurts here.' She pointed to her groin, and clearly the movement hurt her because she grimaced.

'Has it been going on for long?' Madison asked.

'I've had twinges for the last week, but today it's absolute agony.' She dragged in a breath. 'Please—I'm not going to lose the baby, am I?'

'Aches and pains are pretty common in pregnancy and they don't necessarily mean that you're miscarrying or there's a problem with the baby,' Madison reassured her, 'but you've done exactly the right thing coming to see us. Do you mind if I examine you?'

With the patient's permission, she examined Mrs Ellis gently but effectively, then listened to the baby's heartbeat. 'That's nice and strong, so try not to worry too much. The baby's doing just fine. But what we need to do is stop this pain. Do you get the pain all the time, and does anything make it feel worse or better?'

'It's only there some of the time. It's worse when I'm going upstairs or getting dressed or turning over in bed,' Mrs Ellis explained.

Given where the pain was and the description, Theo knew

exactly what the problem was. But rather than muscling in, he waited for Madison, who smiled at Mrs Ellis and squeezed her hand. 'The baby's in absolutely no danger. What you've got is something called symphysis pubis dysfunction—SPD for short. It sounds a lot scarier than it is, and an awful lot of women get it. At eighteen weeks, you're practically halfway through pregnancy, and that's the most common time to start noticing the pain.'

She sat down next to the bed, drew a notebook and pen from her pocket, and sketched a swift diagram to show their patient. Theo liked the way she was managing this: focusing on the patient's worries, making it easy for her to understand. That kind of empathy would make her a brilliant consultant, as Iris had said. And on a personal level…

No. No involvements. He'd made his decision years ago: he wasn't going to settle down, get married and have children. Sure, he dated—he was only human—but he always made sure his dates knew he wasn't able to offer anything long term. If that meant people thought he was a shallow playboy, then fine—he could live with that. As far as he was concerned, other people didn't have to know the real reason behind his decision. He wasn't prepared to put the woman he loved through childbirth, knowing first-hand what could happen when everything went wrong. And no way was he going to go through what his father had gone through.

He forced himself to concentrate on what Madison was saying, just in case she decided to throw a question or two his way.

'Basically your pelvis is in two parts and it's held together by a joint called the symphysis pubis, which is strengthened by lots of ligaments. When you're pregnant, your body produces a hormone called relaxin, which softens your ligaments to make it easier for you at birth—but that also means your pelvis can move during pregnancy, and the movements are what cause the pain.'

'Can you make it stop?' Mrs Ellis asked.

'I'm going to give you a support belt, which will help, and you can take paracetamol to help with the pain—that's perfectly safe for the baby. I'm also going to refer you to a physiotherapist, who can teach you some exercises for your tummy and pelvic floor that won't hurt the baby but will help ease the pain. I can't promise you'll get an appointment with the physio today,' Madison warned, 'but if I can do it, I will.'

'Thank you.' Mrs Ellis wiped away the tears that had started to spill over. 'I was so scared I was going to lose the baby.'

'It's always the first thing that goes through your mind,' Madison sympathised, 'but you're going to be absolutely fine. Even better news is that there are a few things you can do to help make the pain go away.'

This was his cue, he thought. 'Why don't I tell Mrs Ellis while you talk to the physios?' Theo suggested.

Her eyes narrowed for a moment, as if she thought he was trying to take over; but then she nodded, clearly realising that this was going to save them some time. 'Is that all right with you, Mrs Ellis?'

'That's fine. I don't mind talking to student doctors.'

She thought he was a student? Well, it was an easy mistake to make. Madison had been planning to bring her fourth-year students with her, and no doubt the emergency department had cleared it with Mrs Ellis first. Theo just about managed to suppress his grin, though as Madison left the cubicle he could see amusement all over her face. Well, he could live with it. Telling Mrs Ellis that actually he was Madison's boss wasn't going to achieve anything other than make her feel awkward and embarrassed—and his patient's comfort was much more important than his dignity.

He talked her through the things she could do to help herself, and was just discussing the birth plan with her when Madison swished the curtain aside, carrying a support belt. 'I'm sorry, Mrs Ellis. The physiotherapy department is completely booked up today—but I've persuaded them to squeeze you in first thing in the morning, just before their list starts. For now, I'm going to show you how to put this belt on and that's going to take some of the strain for you.'

'Thank you so much,' Mrs Ellis said, looking relieved that she wasn't going to have to suffer pain for much longer.

'My pleasure.' Madison smiled at her. 'Do you have any questions, or has Mr Petrakis already answered them?'

'Mr Petrakis said I should put it in my birth plan to make sure I get the most supportive birth position, and it might affect my pain relief. Will I have to have a Caesarean?'

'I'm not going to rule it in or out at this stage,' Madison said gently. 'We'll see how you go. But I will promise you that we'll do the best for you and your baby.'

'Will I get it again if I have more children?' Mrs Ellis asked.

'We honestly don't know,' Theo replied. 'You might not get it at all, or it might be not as severe, or it might be worse. It really, really varies. But the best advice we can give you is to leave a good two years between pregnancies—if you do get SPD next time round and your baby's not walking yet, you're going to find lifting really hard.'

When Madison had fitted the support belt and checked that Mrs Ellis had transport home, she and Theo walked back up to the ward.

'So are you happy that I know what I'm doing, or do you want to supervise me with some more cases?' she asked.

'I wasn't checking up on you,' Theo corrected. 'I wanted to get a feel for how you worked, and I'm going to be doing the same with all the staff. Mentoring isn't just for students, you know.'

She looked surprised. 'What do you mean?'

'Whatever the stage of your career, you need development or you're going to feel stuck in a rut and be miserable. The last department I worked in had a policy of job enrichment, and that worked really well. If you don't already have that here, maybe we can introduce it—and I'll make sure I liaise with Iris, because I want the midwifery team to be happy with any changes we make and they might have some good suggestions, too.'

She smiled at him. 'I like the way you think. I'm going to enjoy working with you.'

A feeling, Theo thought, that was very much mutual.

Even though for the rest of the day he was in clinic and she was in Theatre, Theo was aware of Madison all afternoon. To the point that, when their shifts ended and he found himself in the locker room at the same time as her, he said, 'Come and have a coffee with me.' Seeing a slightly nervous look on her face, he added, 'Look, I don't mean coffee as in a date. I know you're involved with the guy in the emergency department.'

'The guy in the…?' She looked mystified for a second, then smiled. 'Oh, you mean Ed.'

'The one who called you down to Mrs Ellis,' he confirmed.

'I'm not involved with Ed.'

'Then you're free.' Even though he knew he ought to be sensible about it, he couldn't help mentally punching the air. And then he caught the expression on her face. 'To take pity on the new boy, that is,' he said swiftly. 'I've spent the last five years working in the Midlands, so I don't know the area at all, and I could do with someone to show me where I can get some good coffee around here.'

She shrugged. 'The hospital canteen's OK.'

'They do espresso?' he checked.

'Oh. You mean *serious* coffee.' For a moment, he thought she was going to give him the brush-off. Then she smiled. 'I know the perfect place.'

She led him to a small café not far from the hospital. 'Giovanni's—it's Italian?' he asked.

She nodded.

'A little family place. Sounds good to me.'

'Actually, it's a chain,' she corrected. 'But it's a good one. And I'm very glad there's a branch just round the corner from the hospital. They do the best coffee in London—not to mention these fantastic organic chocolate brownies.'

She ordered a frothy cappuccino and a brownie, and shook her head when he ordered a double espresso. 'That much caffeine is seriously bad for you, Theo. How on earth do you sleep?'

'I'm used to it.' He smiled. 'Espresso is the nearest I can get to Greek coffee outside home. Unless you happen to know a decent Greek restaurant around here?'

She shook her head. 'I'm afraid Greek coffee is a taste I haven't acquired. It's all the *bits*.' She grimaced. 'That thick gloopy stuff at the bottom.'

He laughed. 'You're not supposed to drink it to the last drop. And the *kaimaki*—the froth—is gorgeous, if it's made properly. Like an espresso. But I admit it's an acquired taste, and I can't drink it sweet, the way my father does.' He paused. 'I enjoyed working with you today. You're as good a doctor as you are a dancer. Intuitive and empathetic.'

To his pleasure, her eyes widened slightly. So she wasn't entirely indifferent to him, then? She felt this same weird pull, the chemistry between them?

'Thank you.' She inclined her head. 'I'm sorry I didn't get the chance to thank you for the dance at the ball.'

He shrugged. 'Your friend was rather—how should I say?—*intent* on seeing you.'

She rolled her eyes. 'Put it down to too much champagne. On his part, not mine.'

'I hear you organised the ball. And that you made enough for half a scanner.'

'Only the first half of it.'

'That's still a pretty big achievement.'

She shrugged it off. 'I was part of a committee.'

'But the ball was your idea?'

'The music was.' She grinned. 'One of these days I'm going to convert these philistines and make them admit that the old songs are the best.'

'So you don't like modern music?'

'I just like something I can sing along to. The kind of stuff that puts a smile on your face when you hear it because it's so full of verve. And I don't care if people think it's old-fashioned: I like it.' She took a sip of her coffee. 'I suppose it's because it's the stuff I grew up with. Dad always had it playing in the garage when he was tinkering with a car. Dean Martin, Frank Sinatra, that sort of stuff.'

He couldn't help smiling. 'So would I be right in guessing that your favourite films are musicals?'

'Absolutely. You can't beat a good Gene Kelly film,' she said, smiling back.

The more Theo talked to Madison, the more he liked her. Felt a connection with her. Wanted to spend time with her. Which made her dangerous. He should stop this right now. Apart from the fact that he was only here for six months, he knew that mixing work and relationships could make life much too complicated. And he wasn't looking for a relationship in any case.

Yet his mouth seemed to have other ideas.

'I won something pretty stunning on the tombola—a balloon flight at sunrise. Why don't you come with me?'

She went very still. 'Are you asking me on a date?'

This time his head managed to overrule his heart where his mouth was concerned. 'I'm asking you as a colleague and potential friend,' he said.

She smiled. 'Then thank you. I'd like that. I've never been in a balloon.'

'Then let's synchronise our off-duty. When are you free?'

She took her diary from her handbag. 'Thursday or Friday?'

'Not this week. How about next week?' he suggested.

'Tuesday and Wednesday.'

'Wednesday it is,' he said. 'I'll book the flight and find out what we need to know.'

CHAPTER THREE

THE night before the balloon trip, Madison couldn't get to sleep.

She must have been crazy, agreeing to this in the first place. Quite apart from the fact she wasn't a morning person and she'd arranged to meet Theo at the crack of dawn, Theo Petrakis wasn't relationship material.

Sure, he ticked all the boxes. He was an excellent doctor, kept the team working beautifully together, and his calm, confident manner on the ward managed to calm even the most nervous parent-to-bc. And, as just about every female in the hospital would attest, Theo Petrakis was drop-dead gorgeous.

But he was only here on secondment, covering Doug's sick leave for six months or so. Then he'd move on, and Madison was perfectly happy here in London.

She'd already made the mistake of rushing into a relationship without a future, and she had no intention of repeating it and letting her world fall apart all over again.

All the same, she couldn't get Theo out of her head. Those dark eyes with the unexpected green and gold glints—eyes that always seemed to be full of sunshine. That incredibly sexy smile. The dark hair, brushed back neatly from his face, that made her want to slide her fingers through it and make him look all sexily rumpled. His incredibly gorgeous mouth…

And even though it had been a week and a half since the ball, she could still remember exactly how his lips had felt against the pulse point in her wrist.

'Stop being ridiculous and go to sleep,' she told herself loudly, plumping her pillow and keeping her eyes firmly closed, even though she felt wide awake.

A feeling that didn't last when her alarm shrilled at an unearthly hour. She had to hit the snooze button three times before she could drag herself out of bed, and she was only just ready when the doorbell rang.

'*Kalimera*, Maddie. Good morning.'

Oh, lord. Theo always wore a suit, shirt and tie at work under his white coat. In jeans, a sweater and a black leather jacket, he was absolutely stunning. Touchable.

And she really, *really* wanted to touch.

She hadn't felt a pull this strong since Harry. And that in itself was a warning: look where that had got her. She pulled herself together and unglued her tongue from the roof of her mouth. 'Good morning, Theo.'

'Ready?' he asked with a smile.

She nodded. Theo had given her the pre-flight instructions from the balloon company: to wear long sleeves and trousers, preferably in natural fibres; a hat to protect her head from the radiant heat of the burner; and sensible shoes. And although she felt slightly frumpy, wearing a thick fleece over one of the strappy camisole tops she favoured outside work, she understood the logic, and she didn't want to scrape her arms on the wicker basket.

'Let's go, then.'

She locked the front door behind her and walked with him to the tube station. It was still dark outside, and so early that the train was practically empty, apart from a couple of bleary-eyed commuters who looked as if they still wished they were in bed.

'So are balloon flights always this early in the morning?' she asked.

'Apparently the air's at its most stable in the first two hours after dawn and the last two hours before dusk,' Theo told her. 'So most flights are around sunrise or sunset. The ones over London are at sunrise, though we could have gone for a different take-off point and had a later flight.' He smiled. 'I take it that you're an owl rather than a lark, then?'

'Usually,' she admitted. 'Though I'm never late for my shift.'

He laughed. 'Hey. We're not at work now.'

'No.'

'But since you've got my head back in doctor mode, there's something I forgot to ask you—do you have any medical condition that means you shouldn't fly?'

'I'm disgustingly healthy,' she said.

'Good.' He paused. 'I'm sorry, this is a very personal question...but there's no chance you could be pregnant?'

She felt the colour wash into her face. 'No.' She hadn't actually slept with anyone for two years—and she'd regretted that. Not that she was going to admit either fact to Theo.

'OK. And I'm sorry I offended you.'

'No offence taken.' Though there was one problem. Because of what he'd asked, she was thinking about sex. Specifically, sex with him. Which her common sense told her would be a very bad idea, although her libido was turning a series of cartwheels at the thought.

In accordance with Theo's instructions, they reached the meeting place near Tower Bridge at a quarter past six for the pre-flight briefing. Madison's attention was caught by the balloon itself. An enormous wicker basket with six rigid poles going up to hold the burner, and then the most enormous piece of...what? Silk? Nylon? She had no idea. But it was fascinating to watch the balloon flight team putting everything together and inflating the balloon, first with a fan and then the flames shooting into the mouth of the balloon to warm the air and make the balloon envelope rise.

When the balloon was finally upright, the pilot put the instruments and maps on board, and then it was time for the passengers to board. As they drew closer, Madison realised just how big the basket was. How deep. And, not for the first time, she wished she'd inherited the family height gene like her cousin Katrina, rather than being the shortest member of the family.

'Want a hand in?' Theo asked.

Part of her wanted to stand on her dignity and say, no, she could manage. But the sensible side of her knew what that would mean: a head-first, embarrassing dive into the balloon—even if she managed to negotiate the footholds. 'Thank you. That'd be good,' she said.

'I apologise in advance for the caveman bit,' he said, and scooped her up into his arms; she was forced to slide her arms round his neck for balance until he sat her on the edge of the wicker basket. Then she twisted her legs round and slid into the basket.

'Thanks. I think even high heels wouldn't have been enough to help me climb in,' she said brightly, trying to keep her mind off the fact that she'd just had her arms round his neck and his body had been very, very close to hers.

'Apart from the fact they wouldn't be sensible footwear.' Theo looked all the way down her body. Head to toe and then back again to meet her gaze. And the sultry look in his eyes made Madison's heart beat just that little bit faster.

It was noisy in the balloon, with the burners still heating the air inside the balloon envelope—and then she realised that they were off the ground. Considerably off the ground.

She blinked. 'Wow. I was expecting it to be—well, bumpier than this,' she said. 'Like being on a boat going out to sea.'

'We're moving with the wind, so that's why we can't feel the currents. And a passenger basket this size is really, really stable. It shouldn't rock or sway at all.'

'Either you've done this before or you looked it up on the Internet.'

'Both,' he admitted. 'I was in Australia last year and took a trip across the desert at sunrise. The sand was red and there were kangaroos bounding along, and as the sun rose the light turned all the grey saltbush to green. It was incredible.'

'Sounds it. Mind you, so is this. London in the early spring—look, you can see all the trees starting to turn green over again.' She looked down, keeping her hands firmly on the edge of the basket. The burners had gone off again, and they were just floating in the air. Everything around them was still and silent. She could hear the sound of traffic below, and gulls squawking over the Thames.

'I've never seen London like this before,' she said softly. 'Even going on the London Eye is nothing compared with this. Thank you so much for sharing this with me, Theo.'

The burners sprang into life again, and Theo was forced to bend closer to her so his mouth was close enough to her ear for her to hear his reply. 'My pleasure. Though, as one of the main organisers of the ball, you're the best person for me to share it with anyway. You deserve a treat for all that hard work.'

'Maybe.' She rested her hands on the rim of the basket and looked out as the pilot pointed out more landmarks. Theo was standing behind her, and it felt natural for him to be looking over her shoulder, his hands resting against the basket on either side of hers. And even more natural for her to lean back slightly against him.

The gap between their hands narrowed imperceptibly, and he moved slightly closer, cradling her body against his. And she wasn't sure which of them moved first, but then her left hand was covering his, and his right hand was covering hers, and she was aware of every nerve end in her skin.

'Would you like me to take a picture of you together?' one of the other passengers asked.

'Thank you. That would be lovely.' Theo fished his mobile phone from his pocket and set it to camera mode before handing it to her.

'Stand a bit closer together—I can't quite get you both in.'

Theo stood behind Madison and slid his arms round her waist, pulling her back against him.

'Now, smile.'

Smile, when her knees had just melted and her temperature had risen about ten degrees? But she managed it. Just.

The woman took a photograph, and a second 'just in case', then smiled at them. 'You make a lovely couple.'

'Thank you,' Theo said.

For the return of the phone?

Or for the compliment?

Maybe they'd just hit a patch of particularly thin air, because she definitely couldn't think straight. 'Thank you,' she mumbled.

Theo stayed close to her for the rest of the balloon trip. And although they'd been warned that in four out of five flights the balloon landed on its side, and they'd braced themselves for the impact, she still wasn't prepared for the fact that the basket tipped over and she landed on top of Theo.

Full length.

Plastered against him.

His arms automatically came round her. It was the obvious thing to do, to keep them stable—but then again he'd spent most of the balloon ride with his arms round her.

If she lifted her head from his shoulder, she was close enough to kiss him.

And if they hadn't had the other passengers from the balloon and the pilot with them, she knew she would have done it. Teased that gorgeous, sexy mouth until he was kissing her back and his hands were sliding underneath her fleece and her camisole to encounter bare skin. And she would've been just as quick to rip his clothes off.

Oh, lord.

She could feel her face burning, but Theo didn't make any comment. He merely joined the others in helping to roll up the surprisingly heavy balloon and loading it into the back of the Land Rover that had followed the balloon across London to Alexandra Palace and obtained clearance for them to land.

'So, did you enjoy your first balloon ride?' he asked as they walked through the park towards the tube station.

'It was amazing. I've lived in London for twelve years now, but it's made me see the city with new eyes. There are so many places I haven't explored.'

He waited a beat. 'Maybe we could explore them together,' he suggested.

It shocked her how just much she wanted to agree. 'Maybe,' she said.

When they were sitting on the tube, he slanted her a look. 'Are you doing anything special for the rest of the day?'

'Does an appointment with an ironing board and a pile of laundry the height of K2 count?' she asked wryly.

'That,' he said, 'doesn't sound like fun. How about having lunch with me first?'

'As long as you let me pay,' she said. 'My treat—seeing as you shared your prize with me.'

He smiled. 'I didn't mean in a restaurant. I don't live far from a tube station. Come and have lunch with me.'

Go to his home?

She'd have to be crazy, especially given the way her body

had reacted to his on the balloon. 'It's a bit early for lunch.' It was barely eleven.

He shrugged. 'We were up early. I'd say it's lunchtime.' He raised an eyebrow, as if challenging her. He couldn't make it any clearer that he thought she was being a coward.

Well, she wasn't. 'Lunch,' she said, lifting her chin, 'would be lovely.'

'Good.'

He unlocked the front door of a tiny Victorian terrace with a pocket-handkerchief-sized front garden. The décor was neutral—which she'd expected from a rented house—though a brief glance into the living room as she passed the open door showed framed photographs clustered on the mantelpiece. So clearly he was trying to make the place home rather than just somewhere to live.

'Anything I can do to help?' she asked.

'You can put the kettle on, if you like.' His eyes glittered with amusement. 'Don't worry—I have English coffee.' He retrieved a cafetière and a bag of ground coffee from the cupboard above the kettle, and sliced open the seal. 'If I was going to make proper coffee—the way *I* drink it—I'd use a *briki*.' It must have shown on her face that she didn't understand, because he said, 'It's a Greek coffee-pot—you use it straight on the stove.'

He'd already removed his jacket and hung it on the newel post, but now he stripped off his sweater to reveal a white V-necked T-shirt. One that clung in all the right places.

He'd looked hot in a suit. Gorgeous in that leather jacket and sweater. But now, in jeans and that white T-shirt, he was completely edible.

Madison only just stopped herself touching him.

But no way could she keep her fleece on. She was melting as it was. 'It is OK if I put my fleece on top of your jacket?'

'Sure. Now, let's see.' He was rummaging in the fridge and stacking a pile of ingredients on the worktops. 'Anything you don't eat or you're allergic to?'

'I like all food.' As long as she didn't have to cook it.

'Good. So we'll start with toasted pitta and hummus, then chicken and salad.' He handed her a bottle of milk. 'No sugar for me, please.'

It felt oddly domestic, making coffee for them both while he chopped salad. She'd never done this with Harry. Then again, she and Harry had hardly ever been at home together. They'd nearly always eaten out, neither of them being particularly fond of cooking. 'Anything else I can do to help?' she asked when she'd filled their mugs, added milk and returned the bottle to the fridge.

'You can lay the table in the dining room, if you like. The cutlery's in the top drawer and plates are in the cupboard next to the kettle.' Meanwhile, he was whisking lemon juice and olive oil and fresh herbs in a bowl as if he were a born chef.

She collected the cutlery and went through to the dining room. There was a small dining table with four chairs, and a computer table with a desk lamp and laptop; next to it was a bookcase, stuffed with textbooks she recognised and other books that were printed in Greek and could have been anything from medicine to poetry. There were more photographs on the mantelpiece and a stunning watercolour of a Mediterranean seascape.

She'd just finished laying the table and was about to take a closer look at the photographs when Theo walked in, carrying a plate with hot pitta bread and a bowl of hummus.

'Lunch. And I'm really ready for this. Must be the fresh air.' He gave her another of those knee-buckling smiles.

The hummus was good—to the point where she suspected it probably hadn't been bought from the deli counter of the local supermarket. And when he brought in the next course—

a salad of cucumber, tomatoes, olives, red peppers and salty feta cheese, to go with chicken he'd marinated briefly in that dressing before grilling it—she knew for sure that he'd made it himself.

Theo Petrakis was simply gorgeous. Body, mind and heart—she'd seen him in action in the department enough to know he was kind and clever. And he was a great cook to boot.

If she wasn't careful, she could really fall for him.

'That was fabulous,' she said when they'd finished. 'You're an excellent cook.'

'That wasn't cooking,' he said. 'That was throwing stuff together from the fridge.' He held her gaze, his dark eyes flecked with green and gold and grey. 'One evening I'll cook you a proper Greek meal, if you like.'

Oh, she'd like. 'Thank you.'

And again her heart felt as if it had done one of those odd little flips. She decided to take refuge in a safer topic: work. 'So where did you train?' she asked.

'With a surname like Petrakis, where do you think?' he teased.

Greece? 'Your English is perfect and you barely have an accent.' Just enough to be exotic. Sexy as hell. 'And England's a pretty multicultural place. So I'm not going to presume to guess.'

'I trained in Greece,' he said. 'But I came to England five years ago. I've been working in the Midlands.'

'Job enrichment?' she guessed.

He shrugged. 'My grandparents are English. I wanted to spend some time getting to know them.'

'You didn't see them much of them when you were growing up?'

'No.'

Something in his tone warned her that this was a sore spot, something to be left alone.

'What about you?' he asked.

'I trained in London, but my family's from Suffolk. My cousin Katrina lives a couple of doors down from me, so if we're on the same shift I see her quite a bit out of work.'

'Is she a doctor too?'

Madison nodded. 'She's in paediatrics. And she's brilliant.' She smiled. 'She's practically my sister, seeing as we grew up together. Our dads have a family business and our mums are best friends.' She paused. 'How about you? Do you have any brothers or sisters?'

'Three younger sisters and a brother.' He went over to the mantelpiece and took a photograph down to show her. 'This is Sophronia—she's the next one down from me. Melina's next, then Thalia, and this is Stefanos.'

She could definitely see the family resemblance, though all had darker eyes than Theo. 'Are any of them doctors?' she asked.

'Just me,' he said. 'Sophronia was trying to be a stay-at-home mum, but she missed her job too much.' He smiled. 'And she's very, very good at PR. So she's gone back part time. Melina's a chef, Thalia's an interior designer, and Stefanos is in his last year of an economics degree.' He replaced the photograph on the mantelpiece.

On impulse, she joined him there. 'And who are they?' she asked, pointing to another photograph.

'Sophie's children—my niece Arianna and my nephew Petros.'

It was a candid shot, clearly taken by someone they knew rather than a posed professional picture, and the smiles on their faces were infectious. 'They're gorgeous,' she said, meaning it.

He was standing close enough for their arms to touch, and a shiver went through her at the feel of his skin against hers. Lord. She couldn't remember when she'd last been aware of someone in this way. Maybe not since Harry.

He must have felt the shiver, because he turned to face her. 'They are,' he said softly. Gently, he touched her cheek with the backs of his fingers. 'So what are we going to do about this, Maddie?'

'About what?'

It was a complete fib, and she knew he knew it. He meant about *them*. About the weird pull between them.

'That night at the ball…I did this.' He lifted her right hand and skimmed her inner wrist with his mouth. 'And then I wanted to kiss you here.' He kissed the soft skin of her inner elbow. 'And here.' He kissed the curve of her shoulder, bare except for the spaghetti strap of her top. 'And…'

She closed her eyes and tipped her head back, offering him her throat. His mouth brushed against it, and heat sprang up wherever his lips touched her.

And when his mouth finally connected with hers, her knees went weak. His mouth was soft and sweet and persuasive, and she couldn't help sliding her hands round his neck, opening her mouth under his to let him deepen the kiss.

Time seemed to stop, and all she was aware of was Theo. The strength of his body against hers, the warmth of his mouth, the seductive flicker of his tongue against hers. She couldn't remember ever wanting anyone this much before, even Harry.

Harry.

That was where everything had gone wrong last time.

Too much, too fast.

And an almighty mess at the end.

When he broke the kiss, she opened her eyes. 'Theo. This shouldn't be happening,' she whispered.

He took one step away. '*Signomi*. I apologise.'

It would be sensible to accept his apology and stop this right now. Except she couldn't. The need was too strong. 'Theo, I… That wasn't quite what I meant.'

'No, you were right in the first place, Maddie. We shouldn't do this.' He dragged a hand through his hair.

It only made things worse because, ever so slightly rumpled, he looked sexier than ever and she wanted him even more. 'I think my blood pressure's just gone up ten points,' she said.

'Mine, too.' He shook his head in apparent exasperation. 'This is crazy. Apart from the fact that I'm only here for six months and dating colleagues is usually a bad idea, I'm not in a position to offer you anything more than an affair. And that's…' He grimaced. 'Well, it's not particularly honourable, is it?'

She didn't quite understand. 'What's so dishonourable about seeing each other?'

'Because,' he said softly, 'usually when you're over thirty, when you start seeing someone you're thinking about settling down. So a relationship doesn't mean just having fun—it means getting to know each other, seeing if you suit each other, seeing if you could be happy growing old together.'

'That makes it sound as if everyone of our age is on the lookout for a life partner,' Madison said dryly.

'So are you saying you don't want to settle down?'

'No. When I meet the right person then I'll want to settle down,' she admitted. 'I want what my parents have—what Katrina's parents have, too. A good, strong marriage. A relationship that will last.' Not like her previous marriage, which had collapsed within six months. She paused. 'But how do you know when you meet the right person?'

He spread his hands. 'No idea. But I'm not looking.'

The word 'dishonourable' filtered back into her head. 'You're already involved elsewhere—your partner's back in the Midlands or in Greece?'

'No.' He frowned. 'Otherwise I wouldn't have asked you to come with me on the balloon.'

Divorced, then, she guessed. 'She hurt you that badly?'

Madison asked. She could sympathise with that—Harry had left her feeling burned and with major trust issues. If Theo had been involved with the female equivalent of Harry, it was hardly surprising that he was equally wary of relationships.

'It's nothing to do with an ex.'

She blinked. 'Perhaps I'm being stupid, here, but if you're not involved with anyone else, what's the problem?'

'I can't offer you a future, Maddie. I don't want to get married and have children. So seeing me would stop you meeting someone else, someone who would be able to give you what you want.'

'And what do you think I want?'

'You've already told me—you want a relationship that lasts. Marriage. And, given the look on your face when I showed you the photographs of my niece and nephew, I'd say you want children as well.'

'It's pretty hard not to get broody, working where we do and getting to cuddle newborn babies every single day,' she pointed out.

'I'm not broody,' he said softly. 'I'm perfectly happy just to be an uncle.'

Considering the expression on his own face when he'd talked about his family and the way he was on the ward, always cuddling newborns… 'That doesn't quite stack up.' The words were out before she could stop them.

'What do you mean?' He was very, very still.

They'd opened up this far to each other, she thought, so she might as well be honest with him. 'You're clearly proud of your family and you spend your working life with pregnant women and newborns. So it'd be logical for someone in your position to like babies and want your own family.'

'I do like babies—*other people's* babies. I just don't want my own.' His voice was flat. As if an old, old pain had crushed it.

So it was more than just a messy divorce, then. And the sudden bleakness in her eyes made her guess exactly what had happened. He and his partner had lost a baby, and the relationship hadn't survived the pain. 'I'm sorry, Theo. I had no idea that…' There wasn't a tactful way to say it, and she didn't want to make things worse for him. 'That you'd gone through something painful.' She rested her hand lightly on his arm, wanting to comfort him. 'I really didn't mean to hurt you.'

'I know. And it's not your fault. It's not something I talk about, so you weren't to know.' He looked rueful. 'But it's the kind of thing you can't talk about. Not without hurting other people. And my family's had enough heartache. I can't…'

Discuss it with them. She filled in the words automatically, and her heart ached for him. 'How about friends?' she asked.

He moved his head a tiny fraction to signify the negative.

'Bottling things up isn't good for you, Theo.' She tightened the pressure on his arm momentarily. 'So if you need a friend—if you want to talk at any time—then you know where I am.'

'Thank you. But I don't like dragging up the past.'

She smiled wryly. 'I know what you mean. I don't tend to talk about Harry either.'

'Harry?'

'My ex-husband. I thought we wanted the same things out of life, but it turned out he didn't. And he didn't want to be the one to tell me. Unfortunately, I found out the difficult way.' That Harry most definitely hadn't been ready for children. And although she'd agreed to wait, clearly he'd felt the pressure. In an attempt to escape feeling guilty about not giving Madison the baby she'd wanted, he'd turned to someone else. And Madison had been the very last to know.

It was Theo's turn to rest his hand briefly on her arm. 'I'm sorry.'

'So am I. You know the old saying, "Marry in haste, repent at leisure"?'

He nodded.

'It's very, very true.' She shrugged. 'So. Yes, I want to settle down. But not until I meet the right one for me. I couldn't bear another divorce.'

His dark eyes were very, very intense. And the silence stretched until he said softly, 'So what are we going to do about this?'

'Be sensible, I suppose. Ignore the chemistry.'

He smiled wryly. 'Easier said than done. I've spent the last week and a half thinking about you. Since the moment I danced with you.'

'I've never danced with anyone before who made me feel as if we were floating on air,' she admitted.

He laughed. 'I'm Greek. It's what we do—dance.'

'And plate-smashing.'

'That, too.' His eyes crinkled at the corners. 'But being Greek means having a sense of rhythm.'

'And how.' The words came out before she could stop them, and she pressed her palms to her face. 'Arrgh. I'm not usually this tactless or outspoken. I didn't mean to say that.'

'But you thought it. Just like I'm thinking it now. There's something between us.'

There had been since the very moment she'd seen him. And she was glad he felt the same way—that it wasn't just her being ridiculous or hormonal or desperate.

But acting on that attraction just wasn't a good idea. Not when Theo was adamant that he didn't want children. They didn't want the same things out of life. She'd been there, done that—and no way would she ever get involved with another man who didn't want children with her, didn't want to share his life with her.

'We'll just have to be grown-up about it. We're colleagues. And we like each other, so we'll be friends,' she said.

'It's a deal,' Theo said. 'And I'm going to walk you home before I'm tempted to do something I shouldn't.'

'No need,' Madison said lightly. 'I've spent the last twelve years living in London, it's broad daylight, and I'm used to being independent.' She paused. 'But I'll help you with the washing-up before I go.'

'No. If you're not going to let me see you home safely, you're certainly not going to be my kitchen skivvy,' Theo said with a smile. 'Go home. And thanks for joining me on the balloon trip. I'd have felt a bit out of place, going on my own.'

'It was my pleasure, believe me. I really enjoyed it.' She retrieved her handbag and her fleece. 'Thank you for today, Theo.' On tiptoe, she reached up to kiss his cheek. 'I'll see you at work tomorrow.'

'*Kalispera*, Maddie,' he said softly. 'See you tomorrow.'

CHAPTER FOUR

BEING colleagues and friends with Theo was easier than Madison had expected—but only because their paths didn't cross that much. She was busy with her students when Theo was busy with clinics, and because she was a relatively senior doctor now, it was rare that they were both involved in the same cases. If she'd needed his advice, she would have asked immediately—no way would she ever put one of her mums or babies at risk—but all the complications were ones she'd come across before and she didn't need his experience.

The only times they really met at work were in the rest room—where they chatted with the other staff as much as with each other—and at the weekly team briefings he'd set up. They occasionally lunched together, but it was usually with their students or junior staff and Theo would use it as an extra teaching session, a chance for the students to ask questions. Every so often Madison would catch Theo's eye and wonder if she imagined the sudden heat in his look, or if she was seeing something she wished was there.

But friendship would simply have to be enough.

Madison was catching up with some paperwork one afternoon in the registrars' office when there was a knock on the door. She glanced up to see Theo in the doorway. 'Hi. What can I do for you?'

He took it as an invitation to walk in, and came to sit on the edge of her desk—not quite close enough to touch, but near enough to send her pulse rocketing. She had to fight to look completely unconcerned and casual about it, because she definitely didn't feel it.

'Our students. Do you do any role-play with them?' he asked.

'I haven't with Sanjay and Nita so far,' she admitted. 'What did you have in mind?'

'A joint teaching session. You as the patient, Iris or Rosie as the midwife, and me there as the consultant to answer questions when our students get stuck on diagnosis or treatment.'

She felt her eyes widen. 'Me as the patient? Why?'

He smiled. 'Well, I'm not going to be remotely believable as a pregnant patient, am I? Unless, of course, I'm a miracle of modern medical science...'

She rolled her eyes. 'Very funny. Actually, role-playing's a great idea because it'll give them a safe way to practise their skills. When did you want to start?'

'Tomorrow at half-past eight—deliveries permitting,' he added. 'If we keep it to fifteen-minute sessions, one case at a time, we've got more chance of being able to do a role-play without being called to a patient, and we're also avoiding information overload for Sanjay and Nita.'

'Agreed. It's a date,' she said with a smile.

'Good. Are you busy tonight?' he asked.

'Not that I can think of. Why?'

'I wondered if you'd like to have dinner with me tonight. We could go to the cinema afterwards.'

It was the sort of thing she loved doing with her female friends.

But dinner and a film with Theo...

It would really, really help if she didn't still feel that pull of attraction towards him. If she didn't remember what it was like to dance with him. If she could forget that moment when the balloon had landed and she'd been plastered against him.

'Thanks for the offer, but I'm not that keen on action movies,' she said.

He smiled. 'And I don't like girly films. But there's bound to be something on that we'll both like. Something where we could compromise.'

Help.

Double help.

If she said no, he'd know that she was having trouble with this 'friends and colleagues' business, that she was finding it tough to fight the attraction between them, and it would push him even further away.

If she said yes… Dinner with Theo would be pure torture. Because it would increase the longing for something she couldn't have.

'Maddie?'

She took a deep breath. 'OK. What time?'

'I'll meet you at your flat at, what, six?'

'Six would be lovely.'

He rang her doorbell at six on the dot—he'd already checked the listings on his mobile phone and come up with three alternatives he thought they'd both like.

'Any of them would be fine by me,' Madison said when he showed her. 'They're all good choices.'

'This one starts at eight, which gives us a chance to eat first,' he suggested. 'And I checked out the local restaurant reviews, too.'

'So you have somewhere in mind?'

'I do, but it depends on whether you like French food.'

'There's very little food I don't like,' she said with a smile.

He took her to a small French-style bistro in Covent Garden. When the waitress brought the menus over, Madison turned straight to the puddings and read the menu from the bottom up. Then she became aware that Theo looked amused.

'What?'

'You're reading your menu backwards.'

'It's called planning,' she explained. 'If one of my favourite puddings is on the menu, then I'll have a lighter main course to make up for the fact I'm having a dessert.'

He groaned. 'Please, tell me you're not one of these women on a permanent diet, Maddie.'

'Not *exactly*.' She wrinkled her nose. 'The thing is, I enjoy food.'

'Good. I loathe eating with someone who counts every single calorie.'

'Actually, I do count calories,' she said. 'I inherited the short gene in the family and I put on weight easily, so unlike my cousin Katrina I can't eat whatever I like and get away with it. And I don't want to spend my entire off-duty in the gym on a treadmill to work off the calories—life's far too short.' Not to mention the fact it had been Harry's suggestion. It hadn't just been the long hours she'd worked as a junior doctor or her longing for a baby that had been a problem in her marriage—it had turned out that her image also hadn't been right for an up-and-coming stockbroker. Short and slender was fine; short and curvy most definitely wasn't. 'So that means compromising a little.'

'There's another solution,' he said. 'You could share a pudding with me.'

She laughed. 'No chance. I'm not polite enough to do that. I'd end up having a spoon duel with you. And I'd win—because I'd play dirty and smack your knuckles with my spoon.'

'Oh, would you, now?' He laughed back. 'But, for the

record, I like you and your curves just the way you are. And I really like the fact that you enjoy food and you're not going to nibble one olive and claim you don't have room to eat anything else that evening.'

'No, that's not me.' She shrugged. 'But I should probably tell you I don't cook.'

'Can't or don't?' he asked.

'A bit of both,' Madison said lightly.

When the waitress came to take their order, Madison ordered the crème brûlée. 'Oh, and the salad niçoise to start with, please,' she added with a smile.

Again, she noticed Theo hiding a grin. 'What?' she asked when the waitress had left.

'Not only do you read a menu backwards, you order backwards.'

'And your point is?'

'I'm not laughing at you, Maddie,' he said softly. 'I'm smiling because it's so refreshing to be with a woman who knows what she wants and is direct about it.'

If only he knew, she thought. Because there was something else she wanted. Something she couldn't be direct about, because she couldn't have it.

Dinner was fabulous, and the crème brûlée with rhubarb and ginger compote was just perfect. The film, too, lived up to expectations.

Theo insisted on walking her home from the tube station.

'You really don't have to. I'm streetwise enough not to get into trouble,' Madison protested.

'I don't care. Where I grew up, men look after women.'

'I'm perfectly capable of looking after myself, Theo. Really. You don't have to worry.'

'Tough. You can argue as much as you like—I'm walking you home.'

In the end, it was easier to agree with him.

'Would you like to come in for a coffee?' she asked as they stood outside her front door.

'I thought you said you didn't cook?'

'I'm not making you Greek coffee.' She smiled. 'And even I can manage a cafetière.'

'Then I accept. *Efkharisto.*' He gave her a slight formal bow.

The first thing that struck Theo about the flat was the absence of pink. Madison was capable and professional at work, yet very feminine at the same time; she wore pink a lot, and he'd even overheard her having conversations about sparkly pink nail polish in the staff kitchen. But there was nothing girly about the décor. It was plain, neutral, relaxing. There was a string of feathery butterflies draped round the mirror above the mantelpiece, but other than that there were none of the fluffy things he'd expected. The kitchen was pure white and chrome—absolutely spotless—and Madison switched on the kettle before taking two mugs and a cafetièrc from the cupboard.

'Come and sit down,' she said, ushering him into the living room.

Theo's attention was snagged by the photographs on the mantelpiece. There was a picture of Madison, her hair loose and blown about by the wind, standing in a garden; next to her was a taller woman with similar colouring who looked enough like her to be her sister. 'That's Katrina, I assume?'

'Yes. In my parents' back garden. These are my parents…' She gestured to a photograph of an older couple. 'And these are Katrina's.'

'Your fathers look very alike,' he commented.

'They're brothers. My dad's two years older than Uncle Danny—Katrina's dad.'

In all the photographs, the groups of people had their arms

round each other or were sharing a smile. They were clearly a very close family; for a moment, Theo felt wistful, missing his own family. The noise and chatter of his sisters, his brother's terrible jokes, his father's deep laugh and his step-mother's gentle nurturing.

They'd adore Madison.

He pushed the thought away. It wasn't going to happen. When he'd found out the truth about his past, the way his mother had died, he'd made a vow that he'd never, ever put a woman through the risks of childbirth. And Madison wanted children. Despite the fact that he'd never felt a pull so strong towards someone, he couldn't act on it. It wouldn't be fair to her. Madison, despite her independence and bubbly exterior, was vulnerable. She'd already had a miserable marriage to someone who hadn't wanted what she wanted out of life; how could he ask her to repeat that? And she wasn't looking for a short-term affair, which was all he could offer her.

He changed the subject. 'This isn't what I expected.'

She raised an eyebrow. 'What did you think my flat would be like?'

'Girly. Full of pink, glittery, fluffy things.'

She smiled. 'I'm thirty, not thirteen.'

'Which doesn't mean a thing. So do I get a guided tour?' he asked.

'Sure. This is the living room, and you've seen the kitchen. I'm on the top floor, so I don't have a garden, which leaves you with the bathroom, here…' She led him into the hallway and opened a door to reveal another restful room, in blue and white with a print of a lighthouse on one wall and a mirror decorated in shells. 'And my room.'

Now, that was more what he'd expected, and he couldn't resist smiling. Madison's bedroom was as girly as it got. Although the walls and curtains and carpets were plain and neutral, just like the rest of the flat, there was a huge pile of cushions on the wrought-iron bed in a variety of textures from soft velvet to smooth silk, some of them embroidered and others with decorative beadwork and sequins. There was a haphazard pile of books on her bedside table—from the designs on the covers, he could tell that they were the kind of romantic comedies his oldest sister loved—but the bit that silenced him temporarily was the string of pink, fluffy lights around the mirror on Madison's dressing table.

'Did you just tell me you were thirty, not thirteen?' he teased, gesturing towards the lights.

'They were a joke present from Katrina. But, actually, I like them. They make me smile. And there's a lot to be said for getting up in the morning with a smile on your face.'

Her blue eyes were lit up with laughter, and Theo found himself wondering why on earth Madison's husband had ever let her down—why he'd been mad enough to let her go. Madison was bright and funny and full of the kind of *joie de vivre* that would light up the life of anyone whose life she shared. If she were his, he'd never let her go.

But she couldn't be his.

Not permanently.

Because she wanted children and he really, really couldn't take that risk.

And it wouldn't be fair to offer her anything less than her dreams.

'Theo?'

She looked worried, so he gave himself a mental shake and smiled at her. 'Sorry. Carried away with thoughts of those cushions—and just how girly you really are, Dr Gregory.'

She spread her hands. 'What can I say? I'm a girl.'

He knew that.

Every nerve end in his body was telling him to kiss her.

And he only just managed to stop himself. Because, once he started, he knew he wouldn't be able to call a halt. Not until he'd undressed her and kissed every inch of skin he uncovered, touching her as if he'd be able to commit the feel of her skin, her scent and her taste to his memory.

'Indeed,' he said lightly, and stepped back out of the doorway. Out of temptation. And the best thing he could think of to do was to turn the conversation back to work. Something safe. 'Now, about this role-play thing tomorrow…'

CHAPTER FIVE

THE following morning saw Madison in one of the consulting rooms with Theo, along with Iris, Sanjay and Nita.

Swiftly, Theo ran through what they were going to do in the role-play exercise. 'Maddie's our patient, Iris is concerned so she's just called you in, and I'm here if you want to ask questions.' He smiled at the two students. 'This isn't a test and it doesn't matter if you don't know the answers. It's a chance for you to practise your skills, show off what you know, and you've got two experienced doctors and a senior midwife in the room so you can grill us for information if you need it.'

Madison liked the way he'd reassured their students. Nita was already confident, whereas she'd had to work hard with Sanjay to convince him that pregnant women were much more robust than he thought and wouldn't break when he examined their abdomens.

'First question,' Nita said. 'Iris would go out of the room to call us, yes?'

'And I'd brief you outside the room, too, rather than in front of the mum,' Iris said. 'So I'm calling you in to a mum who's thirty-five weeks pregnant with her first baby. There haven't been any complications in the pregnancy so far, but I've just examined her and she's got high blood pressure, the baby's small for dates, and if you palpate the stomach you can feel the outline of the baby very easily. I'm not happy so I've called you in.' She spread her hands. 'So what are you going to do now?'

'Introduce ourselves and reassure the patient,' Nita said firmly. 'Mrs Gregory, I'm Nita Warren and this is Sanjay Kumar. Iris has asked us to come in and see you this morning as part of our clinic. Would you mind if we examine you?'

Theo, who was sitting on the edge of his desk, smiled broadly. 'Well done, Nita. Given that Maddie's happy to be examined, Sanjay, what are you going to do?'

'Well, if Maddie were a real patient, I'd palpate the baby first and ask a few questions,' Sanjay said.

'As I'm not pregnant, we can dispense with the palpations,' Madison said. It felt very strange to be lying here on the couch in the consulting room. Despite the fact she worked with pregnant women every day, she'd never considered pregnancy in relation to herself before.

Supposing she were expecting a baby? And Theo, instead of being here as a doctor, was sitting by her side, holding her hand, the anxious father-to-be?

She shook herself. That was the most ridiculous fantasy she could ever have imagined. Theo didn't want a permanent relationship, and he'd made it very clear that he didn't want babies of his own. No way would they ever be sitting in a maternity department together as anything other than colleagues.

But no matter how hard she tried to push it away, the idea stayed put.

And what worried her even more was the fact that she actually *liked* the idea. A nebulous thought about having babies someday had sharpened into focus. A baby, with her own dark wavy hair and Theo's beautiful eyes…

Oh, lord. She really had to get a grip. She was supposed to be role-playing a patient with oligohydramnios, not fantasising about something that absolutely wasn't going to happen. 'OK, Sanjay. As Iris told you, you can feel the baby's outline very easily, you already know my blood pressure's up, my temperature and pulse are both normal, and Iris has already done the dipstick test so there's no protein or sugar in my urine. So what are you going to ask me?'

'Have you noticed any change in the way the baby moves and how often, Mrs Gregory?' Sanjay asked.

Good call. She smiled encouragingly at him. 'Call me Maddie, please. The baby isn't moving as much as normal, no. It's been like this for three or four days—that's why I called my midwife and she told me to come in.' Madison was beginning to enjoy herself. This had definitely been one of Theo's better ideas, and maybe they could do this with some of the junior staff as well as the students, to help prepare them for the less common emergencies.

Just as long as she could keep the fantasy of actually being pregnant out of her head. Yes, she wanted a child—but Theo didn't. End of story. It wasn't going to happen.

Sanjay and Nita exchanged a glance. 'We'd get to see her file first?' Nita asked. 'Because in this case I'd want to see the ultrasound results and check the size and position of the placenta.'

'And I think we need to do a physical exam to check that there's no leaking of amniotic fluid,' Sanjay added.

'Why?' Theo asked.

'Because if you can feel the baby that easily and it's small for dates, the amniotic fluid might be on the low side,' Sanjay said. 'Which means the baby's at risk.'

'Good. Why?' Iris asked.

'Because amniotic fluid protects the baby against infection and helps the lungs and digestive system to mature,' Nita explained.

'How can you check the fluid levels?' Theo asked.

'Ultrasound—we'd ask the radiographers to measure the fluid,' Nita said.

'OK, so you've just told me you don't think I've got enough fluid around the baby. I'm worried now. Is my baby going to be all right?' Madison asked.

The students turned to her. 'It's quite common towards the end of pregnancy,' Nita said, 'so try not to worry. But we do want to send you for an ultrasound so we can check the fluid levels and see how the baby's developing.'

'So there's something wrong with the baby?'

'There are all sorts of things that could cause you to have low amniotic fluid. If it's summer and it's been really hot and you haven't been drinking enough, that would cause it. You might have a little tear in the membrane, or if you've had an amniocentesis you might leak a little—the good news is that the membranes can repair themselves if it's a small tear, as long as you get plenty of rest,' Sanjay said.

'And if you're having identical twins,' Nita added, 'there's a condition called "twin to twin transfusion" where one gets a bigger share of the placenta than the other, so one might have too much fluid and the other might not have enough. It doesn't necessarily mean the baby has a problem.'

'But if there is a problem, where's it likely to be?' Madison asked.

'Are you asking as a doctor or as a mum?' Sanjay asked.

'Doctor,' Theo said.

'Kidneys,' Sanjay said. 'Absent, enlarged, or not developing properly.'

'Or it could be a blocked urinary tract, or a congenital heart defect,' Nita added.

Theo smiled. 'Excellent. You two really know your stuff.'

'Thanks to Maddie,' Sanjay said. 'She's been brilliant at spending time with us and talking about differential diagnoses.'

Madison glanced at her watch. 'Thanks for the compliments, guys, but we're running short on time. Now, you've sent me for an ultrasound. The placenta's normal but the fluid's definitely low and the baby's growth rate is poor. You've examined me and the membrane's fine so you don't have to keep monitoring me and the baby for signs of infection. What are you worried about now?'

'Delivery, definitely,' Nita said. 'Speaking to you as a doctor rather than a mum—without enough fluid, the baby's likely to end up in the breech position. And I'd be really worried about cord compression.'

'So would I,' Iris said feelingly.

'So what would you do?' Theo asked.

'It depends on how little fluid there was,' Sanjay said. 'Ideally we'd go for conservative management, keeping a close eye on things and checking the baby's heart rate to make sure he's not distressed, and regular ultrasounds to check the baby's development.'

'But if the fluid's really low and the scan shows the baby's growth is affected,' Nita said, 'we'd have to deliver early. So we'd give steroids to mature the baby's lungs and do a section.'

'What would you notice about the baby after delivery?' Iris asked.

Sanjay and Nita looked at each other. 'Um—lots of vernix because it's early?' Nita suggested.

'Actually, the baby's skin is more likely to be dry and leathery because of the lack of fluid,' Iris explained. 'And the face might look a bit squashed.'

'And because the baby's been compressed in the womb,

you also need to check for club foot,' Theo added. 'Good work, team. Same again on Monday morning?'

'Yes, please,' Sanjay said, smiling.

'Definitely,' Nita added. 'Working with you like this—well, it's made me realise that this is what I want to do when I qualify, Theo.'

'You don't have to make up your mind just yet. You'll have other placements in other departments,' Theo said gently. 'It's lovely to see you both so enthusiastic, but don't close yourself off to other opportunities just yet.'

'I was wondering,' Nita said, shifting from foot to foot, 'if I could ask your advice about my next placement.'

'Sure. We could have lunch today, if you like. Maddie, you're free as well, aren't you?'

'Emergencies permitting, yes.'

Theo smiled. 'That goes for me, too, so you might end up with just Maddie or neither of us. But we'll fit something in.'

'Thanks.'

'Now, I have clinic—and you two are with the gynae team today, aren't you?' Theo asked.

Sanjay glanced at his watch. 'Yes, and we'd better be on time. Thanks for today, Mr Petrakis.'

Iris and the students disappeared; Madison was about to go to her own clinic, but Theo caught her hand. 'Promise me something,' he said.

'What?'

'If you can't make lunch today, page me early so I can make an excuse.'

She frowned. 'Why?'

'Because I don't think it would be a good idea to have lunch on my own with Nita,' he said softly.

She knew exactly where he was coming from. She'd seen the way the student looked at him, too. 'You're the consultant. All you have to do is tell her you're not allowed to date students.'

'So I meet her for lunch and tell her I'm not interested in a date.' He raked a hand through his hair. 'Which makes me sound like an arrogant bastard who thinks anyone female will be desperate to go out with me.'

She laughed. 'Theo, all the single women in the hospital want to go out with you. Do you have any idea how many of them have asked me to lunch and grilled me about you?'

He looked surprised. 'Why would they grill you?'

'They want information so they can work out how to seduce you.'

Surprise turned to worry. 'Oh, lord. I hope you've told everyone I don't mix business and pleasure.'

'I did consider telling them you were gay,' she teased.

The concern in his eyes vanished, replaced with laughter. 'And you think people would believe that?'

'Look at the facts. You're easy on the eye—and don't you dare give me any false modesty here, Theo Petrakis, you know you are—you're thirty-five years old and you're single. Which means either you have a major personality defect—and anyone who spends two minutes with you will know that that's not the case—or you're not interested in women.' She spread her hands. 'But if I start *that* rumour, then all the single gay men in the hospital will be calling me with lunch invitations so they can grill me about you.'

He rolled his eyes. 'I suppose at least they wouldn't want to marry me.'

'Don't bet on it.' She gave him a wicked smile. 'You can have a civil partnership nowadays, you know.'

He groaned. 'Madison Gregory, you've got an answer for everything.'

'Nearly.'

'Civil partnership.' He shook his head. 'You are going to have to make that up to me later, *matia mou*.'

'Yeah, yeah.' She waved a dismissive hand.

'Good coffee. Seriously good coffee. And one of these brownies you were raving about. And…'

It was probably her imagination, she told herself, but all the same the look in his eyes made her heart miss a couple of beats. She shook herself. 'Yeah, yeah. Make a list.' She smiled. 'See you at lunch.'

In the end, Theo didn't make lunch. He was called in to try external cephalic version to turn a breech baby round for a vaginal delivery, and Madison ended up talking to Sanjay and Nita about different foetal presentations in labour and how to avoid intervention as much as possible. They were both busy in clinic during the afternoon, but later that evening Theo called her. 'Are you busy on Saturday?'

'I'm on an early shift.'

'But you're free when you've finished?'

Say no, the sensible side of her urged. But her mouth wasn't listening. 'Yes.'

'You know we were talking about all the places you hadn't explored in London? I wondered if you'd like to come with me to the Natural History Museum to see the dinosaurs.'

Part of her wanted to go. Part of her knew that the more time she spent with Theo, the more she was falling for him—and, considering he didn't want the same things that she did out of life, that would be crazy. On the other hand, maybe spending time with him would convince her heart that being friends was the best way to go. 'We won't get a huge amount of time there,' she warned, 'but sure. I'd like that. I'll meet you on the steps by the main entrance at four?'

'Fine. See you then.'

* * *

When Madison arrived at the museum on Saturday afternoon, Theo was sitting on the steps, reading what looked like a medical journal. She suppressed a smile. Trust him not to fritter away time. But that was probably how he'd managed to become a consultant at such a young age.

His dark good looks were attracting second glances from more than a few women in the vicinity. Hardly surprising. Theo Petrakis was gorgeous. If only, she thought, suppressing the surge of longing.

'What's this, squeezing in some extra work?' she teased when she reached him.

'Of course.' He closed the journal, rolled it up and stuffed it in his pocket. 'Good day?' he asked.

'The best.' She beamed. 'I had two babies.'

He laughed. 'People are giving you funny looks. You might want to rephrase that.'

She laughed back. 'All right. I helped deliver two incredibly gorgeous babies. And I had a cuddle with both of them. Satisfied?'

'Satisfied.' His eyes glittered with amusement. 'Let's go see the T. rex.'

They wandered around the Natural History Museum, enjoying the animatronic dinosaurs. But then they came to a display of spiders, and Madison shuddered. 'Do you mind if we give this bit a miss, Theo?'

'You're scared of spiders, *kardia mou*?'

'Big ones that drop down on you in the shower and threaten you?' She shivered. 'Of course I am.'

'Don't you think that the spiders are more likely to be scared of you?'

'Scared? Of me? You're talking about big hairy things with legs they wave at you in a threatening manner.' She shook her head. 'They're not scared in the slightest. They're warriors—and they see me as their prey.'

He wrinkled his nose at her. 'Sounds as if you need distracting. Let's go and have dinner. I'll cook.'

'Then I'll provide pudding. We'll need to stop at a supermarket on the way back to your place.'

'Maddie, you don't need to do that. You're my guest.'

She put her hands on her hips. 'I'm not going to cook for you in return. So either you let me contribute in the form of wine and pudding, or I don't have dinner with you. Your choice.'

'And you're bossy,' he said with a smile. 'All right. If you insist.'

'I do.'

'Then thank you.'

They stopped off at a supermarket so Madison could buy wine and some panna cotta. Back at Theo's house, he cooked them a simple meal of grilled lamb with herb butter, new potatoes, carrots and broccoli spears, clearly making up for the richness of the pudding she'd chosen. Strange, Madison thought, how in such a short space of time he'd come to know her far better than her ex-husband had in the whole time they'd been together. If only…

She suppressed the thought. 'So what will you do when Doug comes back?' she asked. 'Are you going back to Greece or applying for a senior consultant's post in England?'

'I haven't really decided yet.' He lifted one shoulder. 'You know, this panna cotta is excellent. Good choice.'

Yet again he'd switched the subject away from himself. In a nice way and with a smile, but Madison was starting to wish that he'd let her close. That he'd trust her. He'd claimed that he hadn't been hurt in a previous relationship, but why else would someone put up all those barriers and keep their work and their emotional life so compartmentalised?

He was making coffee when the phone rang. 'I'll let it go through to the answering-machine,' he said.

But after the beep, there was a pause. Then a formal, *'Kalispera, Theo,'* followed by rapid Greek.

He frowned. 'Do you mind if I take this?' he asked.

'Of course not. I'll just be nosy with your bookshelf,' she said with a smile.

The little Greek she knew was nowhere near enough to follow his end of the conversation—which was also conducted in rapid Greek. She caught the occasional '*ohi*', which she remembered from a holiday phrasebook meant 'no', but that was about it.

'Ne. S'agapo,' Theo said. 'I love you too.' And then he replaced the receiver.

Was he going to tell her who had called? Madison wondered.

Not that it was any of her business. The caller's voice had definitely been female—but she could have been one of his three sisters, or his mother, or an aunt he was close to. And given that she and Theo were just friends, she had no right to feel jealous.

The fact that she did feel jealous…well, that was just ridiculous.

Theo flung himself onto the sofa beside her. 'One of these days, I am going to strangle my parents.'

She blinked. 'Any particular reason why?' she enquired mildly.

'I just wish they would stop trying to fix me up with someone.'

She smiled. 'Tell them you're a big boy and you can do it yourself.' The fact it wouldn't be with her… She pushed the thought away.

'Do you have any idea what a Greek family is like?' He stood up again, raking a hand through his hair, and started to pace from one side of the living room to the other. 'Apart from the fact that we give our older generation rather more respect than you do here in London, there's this relentless pressure to settle down, and when I lived in Greece they were forever setting up big dinner parties where I was introduced to some suitable girl.' He shook his head. 'I thought maybe moving countries would give me some space but, no, they have the daughter of a friend arriving in London and would I be so kind as to show her around?'

'Maybe they just thought it would be nice for her to hear a familiar voice in a strange land,' Madison pointed out.

'More like they're shoving yet another potential bride at me. They've been trying to marry me off for years.' He was still pacing. 'I told them, no, I'm a doctor and I have responsibilities—and although I might not actually be at the hospital all the time, I could be on call and have to go in if there are complications. I cannot let my patients down. I love my family,' he continued, 'but they drive me crazy.' He rolled his eyes. 'I suppose I should be grateful that they let me off being in the family business. As the eldest son I should have followed in my father's footsteps.'

Was he actually going to tell her something about his family? 'What does he do?' Madison asked carefully.

'He's in the leisure industry.' He shrugged. 'But I always knew what I wanted to be and my parents never stood in my way.'

'So maybe they don't really expect you to settle down.'

He smiled thinly. 'Unfortunately, they do. Hence the string of potential brides. If I'm not going to be in the family business, the next best thing is that I marry someone who'll be in the family business in my stead.'

She frowned. 'But your sisters and brother aren't.'

'My sisters are,' he corrected. 'And my brother will be, when he graduates.'

She remembered what he'd told her about them when he'd

shown her the photographs. A PR consultant, an interior designer and a chef. Where did that fit in with leisure? But she knew there was no point in asking Theo. He'd probably already let slip a lot more than he'd intended.

Theo glanced at Madison as he paced the room. He really wasn't being fair to her. Here, in London, his background wasn't an issue. She saw him as Theo the man, the doctor, not the heir to the Petrakis hotel chain. And it wasn't her fault that his family drove him crazy.

He sighed and sat on the sofa next to her. '*Signomi*, Maddie. I'm sorry. I should have explained. My family owns a chain of hotels—little romantic boutique hotels. *Expensive* hotels.'

'So you're telling me you're rich?'

'My family is.' He paused. 'Though I've told Dad that because I'm the only one who hasn't joined the family firm, I don't expect to inherit anything. The others have worked for it, so my share belongs to them. And if he ignores me, I'll divide up my share between them anyway.'

Her approving look warmed him.

'But they still keep trying to set me up with a suitable bride. The daughters of friends who also own hotel chains and whose families are all very involved in the business.' He grimaced. 'It's one of the reasons I left Greece. I'm tired of them trying to marry me off to form a dynasty.'

'You never wanted to be part of the business?'

He shook his head. 'I'm a doctor, Maddie. It's who I am. It's what I've always wanted to be.'

'If they know how you feel and they love you,' Madison said softly, 'then they'll accept it.'

'They do…know how I feel and love me, I mean. And they sort of accept it, but I suppose they're still hoping I'll change my mind and go back to Greece. They miss me.' He smiled ruefully. 'And I miss them.'

'So go back to Greece and make your peace with them. Properly.'

'There's no peace to make.' He shook his head. 'We didn't fight. They knew I wanted to come to England and get to know the other side of my family.'

'Your English grandparents.'

She remembered that? 'Yes. But it's…complicated.'

'And you're a very private man. On the surface, you're all fun and fantastic company. But if anyone gets too close, they hit the barrier you've thrown up.' She smiled wryly. 'I know the rules, Theo. And I'm not going to nag you or push you into talking about things you'd rather not discuss.'

'Even though you want to make everything perfect for everyone?'

'Hey. We all have our bad habits.'

'Maybe you're right. Maybe I *should* talk about it.' He took a deep breath. 'It's messy. And I don't even know where to begin.'

Gently, she took his hand. Squeezed it. 'Don't worry about it being messy. I'm not going to judge you. Talk to me, Theo. It doesn't matter where you start. Just talk to me.'

He was silent for so long she began to think that he'd changed his mind.

And then he spoke.

'You know my mother was English.'

'Mmm-hmm.'

'Her parents didn't approve of her seeing my father. They thought he was a waiter, not good enough for their daughter.' He smiled wryly. 'He was a waiter when he met her, admittedly—but that's because my grandparents owned the hotel and insisted he spend a fortnight in every single job in the business, so he could understand exactly how things worked and what kind of issues the staff faced.' Then his smile faded. 'Dad loved my mother. Really loved her. And she loved him. He married her, even though her parents refused to come to the wedding. When they found out they were expecting me, they were overjoyed.' He swallowed hard. 'And she died giving birth to me.'

Madison's heart contracted. Now at last she understood why he'd been so adamant about not having children of his own, even though he adored babies. She'd assumed that he and a former partner had lost a baby and their relationship hadn't survived the tragedy, but she really hadn't expected this. And if he'd been feeling this way for years and years… Something so deeply rooted he might never be able to let go.

She said nothing, just put her arms round him and held him close. Because giving him a hug was the only thing she could think of to make him feel better.

'Dad fell apart. And he couldn't face seeing me because I reminded him of my mother and everything he'd lost. So my grandparents—my Greek grandparents, that is—looked after me for the first two years of my life.'

'What about your mother's parents?'

'Same as Dad. They saw me as the cause of her death.'

So they'd abandoned him, too? She could have cried for the little boy he'd been back then. Pushed away by those who should have loved him when he had been too little to understand what was going on. 'Theo, that's so unfair. And it *wasn't* your fault.'

He sighed. 'Yes and no. If she hadn't had me, she'd still be alive. Anyway, I don't remember the next bit—it's what Dad and Yiayia told me, years later.'

'Yiayia?'

'My Greek grandmother. Apparently I caught chickenpox

when I was two. I was pretty ill with it, so my grandparents called my father. Made him see me. And from that moment I think he realised that he hadn't lost my mother completely—he still had part of her, in me. So he moved in with my grandparents and me. And then he met Eleni, and she mended his broken heart.' He smiled. 'They got married. And they've been happy together. Though every time Eleni was going to have a baby, Dad used to get really tense. I didn't understand why until just after she had Stefanos—and then, when they were sure he was their last baby, they told me. They thought I was old enough to understand by then, and they didn't want to lie to me about my past.'

'And that's why you became an obstetrician?'

'Yes. So I could stop it happening to another family. I've never regretted having Eleni as a stepmother—she's a sweetheart and I love her dearly—but the idea that my father went through such unhappiness when I was small…' He dragged in a breath. 'I wanted to stop someone else going through that. Wanted to save another child from the knowledge and the guilt that his birth had killed his mother.'

'Theo.' She stroked his face. 'It wasn't your fault. I'm sure if you talked to your dad and your stepmother about it, they'd say the same.'

'How can I drag it all up again?' he asked. 'They've been through enough. I can't discuss it with them, hurt them like that.'

'I don't know them so I can't speak for them, but I know how my family would react—and they'd hate to think you were still feeling so bad about things.'

He shrugged. 'I've come to terms with it.'

No, he hadn't. And her thoughts must have shown on her face, because he said gently, 'Eleni's always treated me as if I were her natural son, not her stepson. I never knew my mother, apart from through photographs and what my father and grandparents told me about her, so it's not that I haven't come to terms with my mother dying. I just don't ever want to put a woman through childbirth. If it went wrong, I don't think I'd ever be able to live with the guilt.'

'Theo, what happened was tragic. And I'm sorry your family had to go through such pain. But dying in childbirth is rare. Really rare. And just because it happened to your mother, it doesn't necessarily mean it will happen to your partner.'

'I'm not prepared to take that risk, Maddie. And you know as well as I do how many complications there can be in pregnancy, during labour and in the few hours after birth.' Gently, he wriggled free of her arms and shifted away slightly.

Putting distance between them again.

He'd let her close, and now she could tell he was panicking about it. So the only thing Madison could do was to give him what he clearly wanted. Space. 'Theo, I'm not going to breathe a word of what you just told me. I'll keep your confidence,' she assured him. 'But I can see that you're feeling crowded. So I'll go now. Not because I don't care, but because I think that space is what you need most right now.' She sucked in a breath. 'Just…you know where I am if you want to talk some more.'

Part of Theo knew that he shouldn't let her go. But he also knew that if he asked her to stay, let her that close, he'd end up breaking his unbreakable rule. He'd want to be with Maddie. And, given that they wanted such different things out of life, that wouldn't be fair. He couldn't rid himself of the fear enough to give her what she wanted, and he definitely couldn't be selfish enough to ask her to give up her dreams for him.

'Thank you. I'll call you a taxi,' he said quietly.

'There's no point, Theo. You live all of ten minutes from the tube. I'll have walked there by the time a taxi turns up here.'

'Then I'll walk with you to the station.'

She shook her head. 'I'll be fine. If you're going to make that much of a fuss, I'll text you when I get home so you know I'm back safely.'

'Thank you. Though I'd be much happier if you let me see you home.'

'Don't fuss. I'm a big girl and I can look after myself.' She stood up. 'Thanks for this afternoon and a gorgeous meal. I'll see myself out.'

And even as Theo heard the front door close behind her, he knew he was making a huge mistake.

CHAPTER SIX

'YOU'RE really down in the dumps, aren't you?' It was more of a statement than a question. Katrina put a plate of lasagne in front of Madison and gestured to her to help herself to salad and garlic bread.

'And that's why you made me comfort food?' Madison smiled at her. 'Thanks, Kat. Have I told you lately that you're wonderful?'

'And so are you.' Katrina put her own plate on the table and sat down. 'Want to talk about it?'

'There isn't much to say.'

'Let me guess. Would it have anything to do with a certain consultant that everyone says is a real Greek god?'

Madison shook her head. 'We're just friends.'

Katrina rolled her eyes. 'Maddie, you're so picky. From what I hear, he's a nice guy and a good doctor as well as being the most gorgeous man to work in the hospital for decades. Maybe you should give him a chance, instead of doing what you normally do—a couple of dates and you decide the guy's too much like Harry and you're not going to take the risk of getting involved.'

'I don't do that.'

'Yes, you do, hon,' Katrina corrected gently.

'Well, that's not the case with Theo.'

'Then what's the problem? You like him and he likes you, so give it a try.'

Madison ate a forkful of lasagne. 'You're a wonderful cook, Kat.'

'Flattery isn't going to get you off the hook.'

Madison sighed. 'OK. I'd like us to be more than friends. But he's only here as a locum. He'll be gone in a few months.'

Katrina scoffed. 'There's bound to be another opening at the hospital or one nearby when his contract ends. Or maybe you could try working outside London for a change.'

'You've got an answer for everything, haven't you?' Madison smiled wryly. 'You're right. That isn't the problem.'

'Then what is the problem?' Katrina asked softly.

Madison stared at her plate. 'He doesn't want kids.'

'Ah.' There was a wealth of understanding in that small syllable. Probably, Madison thought, because Katrina had been the one to help her pick up the pieces when her marriage had crashed spectacularly.

'Maybe he just hasn't met the woman he wants to have kids with,' Katrina suggested. 'When he gets to know you a bit more, he might change his mind.'

'No, he won't.' Madison toyed with her food. 'I'm not going to break his confidence, Kat, but he told me why he doesn't want kids—and I know he's not going to change his mind.' She grimaced. 'You're right in that I don't want to make another mistake like Harry. Theo isn't a liar or a cheat—he's an honourable man and he'd never do to me what Harry did. That's why he's not even having a fling with me, because he says it's not fair to stop me meeting someone who can give me what I want in life.' She blew out a breath. 'I want kids, he doesn't, and with something like that there isn't a way to compromise. So all I can do is be professional. Work with him. Be friends. And that's it.'

Katrina reached across the table to squeeze her hand. 'I'm sorry, hon. I wish I could wave a magic wand.'

'So do I.' Madison lifted one shoulder. 'Don't worry. I'll get over it.'

'You know where I am if you need to talk,' Katrina said gently.

Madison nodded. 'Thanks. And you know it's the same for you.'

Madison was bright and professional with Theo at work, but he was aware of the distance between them—particularly when she seemed to avoid him for the entire week. She was either busy in a committee meeting or seeing friends during her breaks; and on her days off, in the middle of the week, her mobile phone was switched off and she didn't respond to his texts suggesting dinner or a film. She was on duty at the weekend, so there was no chance of seeing her then.

She'd done exactly as she'd promised and given him space.

He should be relieved.

So why did he hate it so much?

By the following Monday, Theo realised that he missed Madison horribly and he was going to have to do something about it. That being without her was like living in a permanent December day, grey and cold. And maybe, just maybe, taking the risk with her would be a hell of a lot better than being without her.

For a start, he owed her an apology for pushing her away. Madison would probably adore a bouquet of pink, extremely girly flowers. Though on the other hand she might consider it too showy, not sincere enough.

So maybe he should make her dinner—with a difference. A dinner made entirely of puddings.

Then he'd give her the flowers. In person, rather than

having them delivered. Or maybe a glittery helium balloon with the words 'I'm sorry' emblazoned across it.

He hoped it would be enough to make her realise he meant it. That he was going to make the effort to face his fears. That he was about to break his unbreakable rule...for her.

Theo didn't see her that morning as they were both in different clinics. Madison was nowhere to be seen at lunchtime—called in to a difficult delivery, he presumed. He planned to spend the afternoon in his office, catching up on paperwork; he'd just ordered the flowers, ready to pick up on the way home, when there was a rap at his door.

He looked up and his heart gave a weird little flip when he saw it was Madison. The urge to run across the room to her and wrap her in his arms was so strong that he barely managed to stop himself.

'Come in.' And then he noticed that she looked worried. Really worried. 'What's wrong?' he asked.

'Sorry to interrupt, but I need a second opinion. Have you come across many molar pregnancies?'

'A few.'

'Good. I need to pick your brains.' She grimaced. 'I've got a mum in and I think it's a molar pregnancy—except there's an amniotic sac visible on the ultrasound.'

'It could be a partial mole.' Either way, it didn't sound good, and it meant one family was in line for heartbreak; and he was disgusted with himself when his second thought was that at least it meant Maddie had to talk to him.

For pity's sake. He was a *doctor*. And, given his family history... How selfish could he get?

He switched back into professional mode. 'What are her symptoms?'

'Spotting—the blood's dark brown—nausea and vomiting. And although she thinks she's about nine weeks, her uterus feels much bigger than it should do for that stage.'

'That sounds very like a mole to me. You're going to need to do an hCG test—blood, rather than urine. Tell the lab you need the results stat, and they should be back in a couple of hours.'

'And if it's a mole, the levels will be higher than expected at this stage?' she asked.

'Exactly.' He liked the fact he never had to spell things out for her. 'Want me to look at the ultrasound?'

'Please.' She bit her lip. 'I'm sorry, I know you're busy.'

'I'm never too busy for my team,' he said gently.

And he was never, ever too busy for her.

Not that he was going to voice that. Right now, he had the feeling it would send her running in the opposite direction. Which wasn't what he wanted at all.

'Did you file the scan?' he asked.

She nodded. 'I can access from it here.'

He logged off and moved slightly to one side, letting her lean over his keyboard, tap in her password and bring up the patient's notes on the hospital's computer system so he could look at the scan.

'It looks like a partial mole to me, so if the blood test confirms it we'll need to do a D and C. I'll book a slot in Theatre. Do the blood test and ask her to go for a walk or read or something until the results are back. Make sure she knows not to eat or drink anything in case we have to do the op.'

'I'll get it sorted.'

'And, even more importantly, does she have someone who can be with her while she's waiting and after the op?'

'I'm not sure. If there isn't anyone…'

'Then do what you have to.' He could guess exactly what Madison's solution would be. The same one he'd choose. 'If it helps, I can cover your clinic.' And he'd sort out his paperwork later. Admin could be done at any time; the patient always, but always, came first. 'This isn't going to be pleasant, Maddie,' he warned. 'I'll come and talk to her with you when the results are back.'

She shook her head. 'It's all right. I can manage.'

'I know you're perfectly capable of managing, but you don't have to do it on your own. At times like this, you need support.' Just like she'd given him support the day he'd finally talked about the misery he'd kept locked away for years. 'It's what friends do,' he reminded her. Even though he was aware he wanted to be more than just friends, now wasn't the time or the place to discuss it.

'Thank you.'

She left his office again, and was back two hours later with the test results. He took one look at them and sighed. 'It's a definite. Come on. Let's go and break the news as gently as we can.'

'Mrs Scott's husband was able to get here within twenty minutes, so my clinic's more or less running on time.'

'I'm not criticising you,' he said softly. 'You run your clinic the way that works for you.' He followed Madison back to her patient and introduced himself to Mrs Scott and her husband. 'You've been feeling a bit off colour for a few days, Maddie tells me,' he said gently. 'And your blood tests, along with your scan, show that you have a condition that we call a partial molar pregnancy. I'm sorry.'

'What does it mean?' Mrs Scott asked, holding her husband's hand tightly.

'It means there was a problem when the egg was fertilised. Normally, a baby gets twenty-three chromosomes from you and twenty-three from the dad, but in a molar pregnancy the dad's chromosomes are duplicated.'

Mrs Scott stared at him, frowning. 'But how can that happen?'

'Sometimes,' Madison explained, 'two sperm can fertilise one egg. Instead of twins developing, just one baby develops—with sixty-nine chromosomes instead of forty-six.'

'So I'm not having a baby after all?' Mrs Scott's eyes filled with tears.

'I'm so sorry.' Theo reached out and squeezed her free hand. 'I know it's a shock, and it's probably the last thing you want to think about, but your health is my priority right now. Sometimes, a few months after a molar pregnancy, the molar tissue grows back again, so you'll need to visit a specialist centre in London for follow-up tests for the next six months.'

'What sort of tests?'

'Blood or urine,' he said. 'They test for the same chemicals as they would in a pregnancy test, so you need to make sure you don't try for a baby until you've had a chance to recover.'

'Grow back?' Mr Scott asked. 'You mean, it's like a cancer?'

'Not quite. It's called a gestational trophoblastic tumour—but the important things to remember are that it's benign and it's curable. If the mole does grow back, we'll have to treat it with chemotherapy,' Theo explained gently, 'but because you have a partial mole rather than a complete mole, it's much less likely to happen to you. When your hCG levels are back to zero, in about six months' time, you'll be able to start trying for a baby.'

Mrs Scott was clearly trying to hold back her tears. 'If we try for another baby…will this happen again?'

'The odds of you having another molar pregnancy are pretty low,' Theo reassured her. 'There's absolutely no reason why you can't have a normal pregnancy next time, and you won't have increased risk of any complications.' He was still holding her hand. 'We'll need to take you to Theatre to remove the mole—it's an operation you may have heard of called a D and C.' Quietly, he talked her through the procedure, explaining exactly what he was going to do. 'I do need to do the operation under a general anaesthetic, so you won't be able to have anyone in Theatre with you, but you'll be able to wait outside the theatre if you want to, Mr Scott.'

'So when does my wife have to have the operation?' Mr Scott asked.

'It's entirely up to the two of you,' Theo said. 'We can do it this afternoon, or if you'd rather wait a day or two to come to terms with everything first, that's also fine.'

'It's a *thing* growing inside me, not my baby.' Finally, a tear trickled down Mrs Scott's face. 'Do it today. Please. I don't want it inside me any more.'

'When did you last eat?' he asked.

'Breakfast. I was too worried to eat lunch, and Maddie told me not to eat or drink anything in case you needed to take me to Theatre.'

He nodded his approval. 'That's fine. Have you ever had any allergies or any reaction to a previous anaesthetic?'

'I've never had an anaesthetic,' she said.

'As with any operation under a general anaesthetic, there are risks,' Theo explained, 'but I'll get the anaesthetist to come and have a chat with you and you'll be able to ask her any questions. And if there's anything else you want to know, Maddie and I are here.'

'And there are support groups that can help when you go home,' Madison said. 'I'll get the numbers for you. You'll be able to talk to other mums who've been through the same thing and who can reassure you that they went on to have a healthy baby. I know right now this is scary because molar pregnancies aren't that common, but the main thing to remember is that it isn't your fault. It could happen to anyone.'

Mrs Scott swallowed hard. 'I just wish it hadn't happened to us.'

'Will Denise have to stay in?' Mr Scott asked.

Theo shook his head. 'There's no reason why you can't go home together afterwards. I would advise you to take at least tomorrow off work, Mrs Scott, and maybe a day or two after—just see how you feel, and be kind to yourself. And do talk to people about how you're feeling rather than bottling it up.'

Theo was telling someone not to bottle things up?

Madison caught his eye briefly, and saw the wry recognition in his gaze—he'd clearly guessed what she was thinking. Definitely a case of pots and kettles.

'We'll send the anaesthetist through to you now,' Theo said. 'And we'll see you in Theatre. Try not to worry,' he added gently.

When he and Madison had left the consulting room, he turned to her. 'Do you want to assist?'

'Is this part of your job enrichment thing?'

He nodded. 'Which isn't me being cruel and heartless, by the way. This is a horrible situation and we need to get something positive out of it—so if it gives you more of an insight into another specialty, that's a good thing.'

'In other words, if life gives you lemons, make lemonade.'

He gave her a half-smile. 'That's a pretty good philosophy. Works for me.'

But did it? she wondered. Because, despite the fact he loved his family and he liked children, he still refused to face his fears. He was still adamant that he'd never get married and have children.

They both changed into Theatre greens and scrubbed up.

'You're probably aware that the risks of the op are quite minor,' Theo said. 'Because of her pregnancy, her uterus is soft, so the biggest risk is perforation—I need to watch for that, and I also need to make sure I remove all the mole and send samples to the lab.'

'All textbook stuff.' She took a deep breath. 'But textbooks don't prepare you for the way you feel, do they? The Scotts really wanted this baby, Theo, and they'd been trying for almost a year. They're completely broken-hearted. And I feel so bad that I can't fix it for them.'

'It isn't your fault, Maddie. And there's no reason why they can't try for another baby in the future.'

How could he say that so coolly and calmly? she wondered. *How*, when he wasn't prepared to face those risks himself?

The operation went smoothly, and after Mrs Scott had come round in the recovery room, Madison brought Mr Scott in to see his wife and sat with them for a while. 'I know Theo talked to you about what to expect after the operation, but you've had a lot to take in so I thought you might find this useful.' She gave them one of the patient advice sheets she'd written the previous year and had updated a couple of months before. 'Don't worry if you have any irregular bleeding, because that's perfectly normal—but if you develop a temperature or you have a tummy ache or you find your period's very heavy and clotty, you need to talk to your family doctor as you might have an infection. Don't use a tampon until your next period, and it's a good idea to avoid sex until the bleeding's stopped.'

'How long will it go on?'

'It varies—a few days. But if the bleeding goes on for longer than that, come back and see us and we'll check you out.' Prolonged bleeding might mean that the molar tissue had grown into the muscle layer of Mrs Scott's uterus—not that she was going to worry her patient with potential complications.

When Madison finally left the ward, she passed Theo's open door; some instinct made him glance up. She looked really miserable, he thought. 'Maddie—a word?' he called.

'Sure.' She walked into his office.

'Close the door.'

As she did so, he got up and walked towards her, then slid his arms round her, holding her close.

She pulled away. 'Theo, this isn't a good idea.'

'I'm merely giving you a hug,' he said softly. 'As I would any colleague who looked as upset as you do right now. As you said to me once, it's what friends are for. And I'm here for you.' He paused. 'Is it the Scotts?'

'Partly.' She sighed. 'It's been one of those days. The radiologist called me down to see one of our mums this morning because the baby's heartbeat wasn't there. I had to explain to her that she'd lost the baby and was going to miscarry over the next few days—and if she didn't, she'd have to come in and be induced and she'd have to go through labour. With no baby at the end of it.' She swallowed hard. 'Days like this, I really hate what I do for a living.'

Theo wrapped his arms round her again. 'Every obstetrician I know has days like this. Ones where we can't help and it makes us wonder what all those years of study were for because we feel so inadequate. And even though we know in our heads that nobody else could have fixed the problem either, it takes a while for our hearts to remember it.' He stroked her hair. 'The best thing you can do right now is to think of all the other days. All the times when it goes right and you're the one who helps bring a new life into the world and hears a baby's very first cry.'

'I know.' She dragged in a breath. 'But, as you said, there's a difference between head and heart.'

Yes. His own head and heart were having one hell of a struggle at the moment. His head knew he should let her go. His heart wanted to keep her exactly where she was: in his arms. Close. Near enough to kiss.

Though now wasn't the right time to put pressure on her or try and make sense of the muddle in his head. He let her go. 'Come on. I'm taking you out for something to eat.'

She shook her head. 'Thanks for the offer, but I really don't think I can face anything.'

'Then I'll make you something at my place. We need to get out of here.' At her surprised glance, he admitted, 'The Scotts have got to me as well. I meant what I said just now. I too hate the days when we can't fix things and make everything all right again. So I think right now you and I need some serious comfort food.'

For a moment, he thought she was going to refuse. But then she nodded. 'OK. Thanks.'

He quickly logged out of the system and shut down his computer, and walked off the ward with her. Just as they reached the exit doors, Theo remembered the flowers he'd ordered. And how inappropriate they were. 'Excuse me a minute, Maddie. I need to make a quick call.' One he didn't want her to overhear. To his relief, she gave him the space he needed, so he rang the florist to explain there had been an unavoidable delay and he'd collect them the following day instead.

'All sorted?' she asked when he'd cut the connection and walked back over to her.

'Yes. Come on, let's go and eat.'

CHAPTER SEVEN

THEO's house was within walking distance of the hospital; he and Madison didn't bother with conversation on the way there, but at least it was a companionable silence.

Madison wondered if she were doing the right thing. He'd held her in his office. Said that he was just doing what any friend or colleague would do.

And it wasn't enough for her any more, being just friends and colleagues.

Because she realised that she'd fallen in love with Theo. The one thing she'd promised herself she wouldn't do since Harry—fall in love with a man who didn't want the same things in life that she did. She'd made the same mistake all over again, even down to falling for a man she hadn't known for very long.

She must need her head examined.

When he closed the front door behind them, she said, 'Theo, this is really sweet of you, but right now I don't think I can face food.'

'Yes, you can,' he cut in, before she could protest further. 'And it will make you feel better, I promise.'

'But—'

'No buts, Maddie.'

He was in steamroller mode and Madison just didn't have the energy to fight him, so she let him shepherd her into the kitchen. He poured coffee grounds into a pan, along with a measure of water, stirred it and set it to boil on the stove while he heated milk.

She blinked. 'You're making us Greek coffee?'

'I'm making *myself* Greek coffee,' he corrected, shaking coffee grounds into a single-cup filter. 'I know you don't like it, so don't worry. I'm not going to make you drink it.'

While their drinks were brewing, he cut doorstep slices from a loaf of multigrain bread and toasted them, then added slices of cheese and put them under the grill until it bubbled.

'One latte,' he said, handing her a mug of coffee made just the way she liked it, 'and cheese on toast. And we're going to eat on the sofa.' He smiled at her. 'It's the best comfort food I know, apart from Eleni's chicken soup.'

'Thanks. That was fabulous,' she said when she'd finished a little later.

'It was common-or-garden cheese on toast,' he replied with a wry smile. 'Nothing special.'

'But *I* didn't have to make it. Which means it tasted even better.'

'Thank you. I think.' He took her plate and empty mug.

'Theo, you don't have to wait on me.' She followed him out to the kitchen. 'And as you cooked, I'll do the washing-up. It'll stop me feeling guilty,' she said, pre-empting the protest she sensed he was about to make.

He shrugged. 'If you insist.'

'I do.'

Except when she was drying up one of the mugs, it slipped from her fingers. And as soon as it hit the ceramic-tiled floor, it smashed into tiny shards.

'Oh, no. I'm sorry. I…'

'It was an accident, Maddie,' he said gently, touching her

cheek with the backs of his fingers. 'Don't worry. It's not a problem. I'll sort it out.'

Within seconds, it seemed, he had the shards swept up, wrapped in newspaper and deposited in the bin.

'I'm so sorry, Theo.'

'Stop apologising. It's all right.' He took her hands and drew her out of the kitchen, then slid his arms round her. 'We've both had one of those days when everything feels out of kilter—and right now I think you could do with a hug.'

She could see the bleakness in his eyes; she had a feeling that he was voicing his own needs, too. So she slid her arms round him, rested her cheek against his chest and held him close. For a moment he seemed to freeze, and then he rested his cheek against the top of her head, letting her comfort him as he was comforting her.

Madison had no idea how long they stayed like that, just holding each other and drawing strength from each other's nearness. And it felt so good.

Though, at the same time, she knew shc was just compounding her errors. The longer she remained in his arms, the harder it would be to leave them.

'I ought to go.'

'No.' He rested his cheek against his hair. 'I've missed you this last week.'

Had she heard that right? 'You missed me?'

He nodded. 'I've missed chatting to you over lunch. I've missed playing tourist with you.'

He meant as friends, she knew. She dragged in a breath. 'Theo. About this friendship thing. I'm not sure I can do it any more.'

'Neither can I.'

She pulled back slightly so she could look him in the eye. 'So what are you suggesting, exactly?'

He surprised her by admitting, 'I've told myself for years that I don't want marriage and children. I don't want to take the risk of losing someone I love, the way my father lost my mother.'

'Even though your dad was brave enough to take that risk with your stepmum?' she asked softly.

He inclined his head. 'I guess I'm a coward.'

'No. Just blaming yourself for something that wasn't your fault.' She reached up to stroke his face. 'Plus there's the fact that medicine's always advancing. We can do things now that we couldn't do five years ago, let alone thirty-five. Maybe if you'd been born now, the obstetrician could've made a difference for your mum.'

'Maybe.' He dragged in a breath. 'I've really missed you, Maddie. This last week, being without you…I've hated it.'

'You said you could only offer me friendship,' she reminded him.

'I was trying to be unselfish. Giving you the chance to find someone who could offer you everything you want—everything you deserved but which I couldn't give you.' He looked rueful. 'But I think I've learned that I'm not always right. That sometimes I can be very stupid.'

'So where does that leave us now?'

'I want you, Maddie,' he said simply. 'And you're the only woman I've ever met who's made me want to break my personal rule.' He raised her hand to his mouth and pressed a kiss against the palm. 'You know that phone call I made?'

She nodded.

'It was to a florist's—I'd ordered some flowers this morning. For you. But after the day we've had, it didn't seem the right moment to give them to you, so I put them on hold until tomorrow. And I was planning to make you a special dinner to apologise. All puddings. Strawberry soup as a starter, pilaf with almonds and cinnamon and apricots for the main course— Oh, and crème brûlée.' His eyes crinkled at the corners. 'Though, given that you order backwards, I should've said that all the other way round.'

He'd planned to do all that for her?

Cook her an entire dinner of puddings?

Just to say sorry?

She blinked hard. 'Theo. I don't know what to say.'

'I've got a better idea.' He dipped his head and brushed his mouth against hers. Softly. Gently. A kiss of warmth and promise.

Then he did it again, this time taking a tiny nibble of her lower lip, coaxing her into a response. And then it was as if something had snapped and the kiss turned hot, his mouth jammed against hers. His arms were wrapped round her, holding her tightly against him, and hers were wrapped equally tightly around him.

Right now, she needed this so much. She wanted him to blow her mind with pleasure, make her forget the horrible day they'd spent at work.

He broke the kiss, whispering something in Greek that she didn't quite catch, and then he drew a trail of hot, open-mouthed kisses all the way down her throat. Madison closed her eyes and tipped her head back, wanting more; right now she needed to be skin to skin with him. She wanted him to take off her top and bare her skin and kiss every inch of skin he uncovered until she was so dizzy with desire that she couldn't think straight.

'I love this colour on you,' he murmured against her ear, his breath fanning against her skin and making her shiver. 'You look great in strong colours.'

Colours? He was kissing her stupid and he could notice what she was wearing? She opened her eyes and stared at him in disbelief. 'You notice colours? I thought only—'

'Gay men did?' he finished, laughing. 'Remember my sister Thalia's an interior designer. After half a day with her you look at things in a whole new way. So, yes, I notice colours. You look fabulous in that.' He nipped her earlobe gently. 'I want to make love with you, Maddie. I've wanted you since the first moment I danced with you at the ball. I've been trying to hold back, for your sake—but I can't hold back any more.' His voice had gone husky with desire, and his accent was just that little bit stronger. Sexy as hell.

'I want you, too,' she whispered.

He slid his fingers under the hem of her top; she could feel the pads of his fingertips stroking the skin of her abdomen, warm and soft and very, very sure of what he was doing.

He dipped his head again and brushed his mouth very lightly against hers in the sweetest, gentlest kiss. Within a second the kiss had turned so hot that her bones felt as though they were melting.

Ridiculous. She knew it was anatomically impossible. But when he kissed her—and she was kissing him back—it felt as though anything was possible. Right at that moment she wanted time to stop so the kiss would last for ever.

It had never been like this for her before. Not even with Harry.

'I know this is a bad idea,' he said as he broke the kiss.

'Actually, I think this is one of your better ideas,' she corrected, cupping one hand against his cheek. 'Right now, we need to celebrate life.'

He turned his face to the side so he could press a kiss into her palm. 'You have a point. Allow me a caveman moment?'

'You had cavemen in Greece? I thought you were all born sophisticated,' she teased.

'We do cavemen—in our fashion.' He raised an eyebrow. 'But if you want sophistication…' He proceeded to kiss her. Thoroughly. Until her knees went weak and she didn't protest when he picked her up and carried her up the stairs as though she weighed no more than a feather.

Once in his bedroom, he set her on her feet—letting her slide all the way down his body, holding her close so that she could feel just how turned on he was and how much he wanted her. Then he swiftly sorted out the curtains and switched on the bedside light. Catching her eye, he said, 'Sorry that it's an ordinary bedside lamp and not a string of pink, fluffy lights.'

She laughed. 'Clearly I need to buy you some.'

He groaned. 'That wasn't a hint or a challenge, Maddie.'

'No?'

'No. And I've got more important things to think about than fluffy lights.'

'Such as?'

He rubbed the pad of his thumb along her lower lip. 'You have a beautiful mouth, Maddie.'

His touch made desire lick all the way down her spine. Spark to a flame. 'So do you.' She imitated his action.

He shivered, then laced his fingers through hers and slowly drew her arms upwards. 'That's better,' he said softly, and pulled her top up over her head. 'Have I told you how beautiful you are?' he asked, his voice husky. He traced the lacy edge of her bra with the tip of one finger. 'Just gorgeous. And I can't believe I've managed to keep my hands off you for so long.'

'You really want me?' She could barely believe this was happening. That he felt the same way she did.

'Oh, I want you.' He dipped his head to kiss the hollow of her collarbone. '*Se thelo.* I want you so much, Maddie. You blow my mind.'

Pleasure rippled down her spine. She affected him that much?

Then again, she reacted in exactly the same way to him.

She reached out and undid the buttons of his shirt. Slowly,

achingly slowly, savouring every moment until she pushed the soft cotton off his shoulders. 'You're beautiful, too.'

He smiled at the whimsy. 'Can a man be beautiful?'

'Oh, yes.' Her nod was emphatic. 'And you are.' He wasn't lean and skinny, but he wasn't fat either—just beautifully toned, with powerful shoulders and strong biceps and narrow hips and strong thighs. He really did look like a Greek god, one of the statues carved lovingly by sculptors in ages past. And the contrast between his olive skin and her own very fair English complexion made her shiver with pleasure.

He responded by sliding the straps of her bra off her shoulders and kissing the bare skin he'd revealed before unsnapping her bra and letting it fall to the floor between them. Then he dropped to his knees and teased her with his hands and his lips and his tongue, stroking her skin and kissing her until she was quivering.

And then it was her turn to touch him, to kneel down next to him and let her fingertips skate over his pectorals and down over his abdomen before undoing his belt and the button of his trousers.

'My beautiful, beautiful Maddie,' he whispered, and unzipped her skirt.

She'd thought that if their control ever did snap and they made love, they'd be ripping each other's clothes off, desperately needing, wanting each other so badly that they couldn't wait. But this slow, deliberate exploration of each other's bodies was even more exciting. Taking the time to explore each other's skin, learning the texture with their fingertips, discovering where a touch would make the other shiver with pleasure and where a kiss could elicit a little involuntary murmur of desire.

When they'd finally finished removing each other's clothes, Theo brushed his mouth against hers. He teased her lips open so he could deepen the kiss, then he picked her up and laid her against the soft down pillows. He stroked her cheek, then kissed his way down her body; he paid attention to the curve of her inner elbow, the soft undersides of her breasts, discovering erogenous zones she'd had no idea existed. And then he started again from the hollows of her ankles and worked his way upwards, feathering kisses against her skin until she was quivering and parting her thighs.

'Theo. Please. I need…' she whispered, sliding her hands into his hair.

The first touch of his mouth against her sex made her shiver. The second made her breath hitch. And when he circled her clitoris with his tongue she couldn't suppress an 'Oh' of pleasure.

The waves of pleasure built and built, until finally her climax hit. And when she'd stopped shaking, she realised that she was in his arms and he was holding her close. 'Better?' he asked softly.

She nodded and reached up to kiss him. 'But I haven't finished yet.' She curved her fingers round his shaft, stroking and caressing until he arched against the bed and gasped with pleasure.

'Now?' she asked.

He opened his eyes; his irises were almost pure gold with pleasure.

This was a celebration of life. A reminder that life could be good as well as bad.

And how.

'Now,' he said.

But as she was about to move over him, his fingers encircled her wrist. '*Nearly* now,' he amended, and reached with his free hand into the drawer of his bedside cabinet to fish out a condom.

Lord, that had been a near miss.

To think that making love with Theo could put her in the state where she actually forgot to be sensible…

'Having second thoughts?' he asked softly.

She knew that if she said she wanted to stop, he'd respect her enough not to push her—despite the fact that he was clearly very aroused. But she believed in being fair. He'd driven the demons away for her. She'd do the same for him.

She undid the little foil packet and rolled the condom over his shaft, then shifted so that she straddled him before lowering herself onto him. He tilted his pelvis slightly so he slid even deeper into her, and his fingers laced through hers as she moved over him.

To Madison's amazement, her climax built again—far more rapidly than she would have believed possible. As she felt her body tightening round his, Theo released her hands, sat up, wrapped his arms round her and buried his face in her shoulder, breathing in her scent.

As the little aftershocks died away, she realised he was still holding her tightly, as if she were the most precious thing in the world and he'd never let her go. For that moment, it felt as if Theo was telling her he loved her—telling her with his body, even though he wasn't saying the words. Though he'd practically admitted it by telling her that tonight he wasn't listening to his head.

She knew how that felt.

She hadn't listened to her head either. She'd let the emotion sweep her away. The way she felt about Theo made her feelings for Harry pale into insignificance.

Because she loved him.

Really loved him.

Heart, mind and soul.

Not that she had any intention of saying so. She wasn't going to be the one to say the words first.

Theo kissed her lightly. 'If you'll excuse me, *hara mou*, I'd better go and deal with this in the bathroom.'

'Sure.'

When he'd left the room, Madison realised that this was her cue to leave. She'd scrambled out of bed and was just picking up her clothes when Theo returned. 'Don't go, Madison,' he said softly. He took her hand and drew her back over to the bed, sitting down and pulling her onto his lap. He raised her hand to his mouth and kissed each fingertip in turn. 'Stay with me tonight.'

'You're sure about this?'

'Very sure.'

He wanted her to stay.

Which would take their relationship to a new level.

And this was the nearest he'd come to a declaration—the fact he wanted her to stay with him told her how much he cared. So she nodded and let him manoeuvre her back into bed with him. He shifted so he was lying on his back, with one arm round her and her head resting on his shoulder; the fingers of his other hand were entwined with hers.

There wasn't any need for words. Right now he was telling her that she was safe. That he would cherish her. That she didn't need to worry.

And slowly her eyes closed and she drifted off to sleep.

CHAPTER EIGHT

THE alarm shrilled—an unfamiliar alarm—and Madison woke with a start. It took a second or two to remember where she was, and then Theo reached over her, switched off the alarm and kissed her bare shoulder. *'Kalimera, kardia mou.'*

'Uh. Morning,' she croaked.

Though it didn't feel like morning.

It felt way, way too early to be morning.

'You're really not a morning person, are you?' She could hear the smile in his voice. 'I'll make us some coffee. If you want the shower first, help yourself.'

Shower.

Work.

Everything snapped into place. Oh, lord. She was at Theo's. And the only clothes she had were the ones she'd been wearing the day before. No way could she go to work in those, even if she'd been thinking straight enough to rinse out her underwear the previous night. The thought was enough to wake her up properly and she sat up. 'Theo, I need to go home and get some clean clothes.'

'Of course.' He touched her cheek gently with the back of his fingers. 'Sorry. I didn't think things through last night.'

She could see the rest of it in his eyes. He'd needed

comfort, just as she had. And she didn't regret staying. Last night, he'd actually let her close. Given her hope that maybe, just maybe, this thing between them would work out.

'I'll run you home,' he said.

She shook her head. 'Thanks for the offer, but even at this time of the morning the rush hour will already have started. It'll be quicker to take the tube.'

'I'll make you some coffee—and I'll add cold water so you can drink it straight down.'

Just the way she did at work. And she knew he'd make it exactly as she liked it. Theo paid attention to detail. 'Thanks. And, um, do you have a spare toothbrush I could borrow, please?'

'Sure.' He climbed out of bed, completely unselfconscious of his nakedness, and headed for the bathroom. When he returned, he sat on the edge of the bed next to her and handed her a toothbrush head. 'I use a rechargeable toothbrush—this is a brand-new head that'll fit on the base.' He looked straight at her. 'I've put a pink marker ring on the bottom of it so you'll know it's yours.'

Her heart missed a beat. Was this his way of saying that he wanted her to stay overnight some time in the future?

He leaned forward and kissed the tip of her nose. 'I'll make that coffee I promised you. Help yourself to whatever you need in the bathroom.'

This time he took a navy towelling robe from the back of the door and shrugged it on as he left the room. Madison collected her clothes from where they were scattered over the floor—lord, they really had been focused on each other last night—and took them into the bathroom. She showered, using his citrusy shower gel; the scent made her think of him and every nerve end tingled at the memory of the way he'd made love with her the previous night. For a moment she actually contemplated going downstairs wearing nothing but a towel and dragging him back to bed.

Then common sense kicked in. They were both due at work. Making them both late really wouldn't be fair on their colleagues or the women waiting for appointments. She dressed swiftly; wearing yesterday's clothes wasn't pleasant, but she reminded herself that it was only going to be for one short journey on the tube. She padded down the stairs to the kitchen; Theo looked up as she reached the doorway.

'Perfect timing.' He handed her the mug of coffee. 'Can I make you some toast, or would you prefer fruit and yoghurt?'

'Do you have any cereal?' she asked hopefully.

He shook his head. 'Sorry. The best I can do you is toast. I could scramble you some eggs, if you like.'

'Thanks, but I'll pass. I'll grab something at my place.'

He waited a beat. 'So where do we go from here?'

'I don't know.'

'The way I see it, we have three choices. One, we can forget last night and go on as we were.'

His expression was unreadable, and a chill ran down her spine. Was that what he wanted? 'And the other options?' she asked carefully.

'Two, we face it that last night happened but we realise we don't have a future, and make a clean break. From now on, we'd be colleagues only.'

Oh, lord. This was getting worse. 'And three?'

'Three…' He dragged in a breath. 'Three, we see if we can make a go of this.'

Was that a real possibility? She looked straight at him. 'What do you want?'

'I'm torn between my heart and my head,' he admitted. 'I've always said that settling down—the whole marriage and children thing—wasn't for me. But I broke the rules last night.

You're the first woman I've spent the entire night with since I was a student.'

She blinked, trying to take in what he was saying. 'You were celibate that long?'

He smiled wryly. 'No, but I only dated women who didn't want a proper relationship—who wanted fun and no commitment. Which meant never staying the night with them.' He paused. 'What do *you* want, Maddie?'

She owed it to him to be honest. 'I want someone who's going to love me for my own sake. Who wants the same things out of life as I do.'

'So we're back to kids versus no kids,' he said quietly.

'There are alternatives. Adoption. Fostering.'

'And you'd be prepared to give up having a natural child?'

'It's an option,' she said carefully. 'Something to think about.'

He nodded. 'The thing is…if we make a go of this, we're going to make love. A lot. And no matter how careful we are with contraception, you know as well as I do that the only one hundred per cent guaranteed contraception is abstinence.'

She followed his drift. 'So even if we didn't plan children, I could still get pregnant by accident.' And she knew that would really freak him. Big time.

He sighed. 'We haven't really got time to discuss this properly now. But maybe we can grab a sandwich at lunchtime and take it to the park or something, find a quiet corner.'

'Babies permitting.'

'Babies permitting,' he agreed with a smile.

She took a sip of the coffee and realised with relief that he'd made it as promised, so she could drink it straight down. She drained the mug, then rinsed it under the tap. 'I'd better go, or I'll be late for clinic.'

He kissed her lightly. 'See you at work.'

Back at her flat, Madison changed swiftly and grabbed a

quick bowl of cereal. All the way to the hospital her head was full of the previous night—and what Theo had said that morning.

He wanted her. She knew that. Maybe even loved her, because he'd told her she was the first one he'd let this close to him in years. But would that be enough to get them through their differences, help them find a way of compromising?

Theo spent the morning in clinic. Reassured every single one of his high-risk mums-to-be, examined bumps and checked foetal heartbeats and double-checked blood pressures and persuaded one that she really needed to spend a day or two on the ward on bed rest, where they could keep an eye on her, and reassured another that it didn't matter that she had a low-lying placenta because as the baby grew the placenta would move away from the cervix and there was every chance she could have a normal birth.

He was on the way back to the ward, walking past the room where he knew Madison was holding her own clinic, when the door opened. He saw her talking to the pregnant woman in the doorway and noticed that she was using exaggerated lip movements. She didn't usually use her hands as much as that when talking. And then he caught the other woman's intonation and realised that she was deaf. Madison was clearly using sign language, something he really hadn't expected.

Then again, his life had been full of surprises since he'd first met Madison.

'Hey, there. Finished clinic?' Her voice cut into his reverie.

He smiled at her. 'Yes.'

There was a flash of heat in her eyes that triggered corresponding heat all the way down his spine. Oh, lord. How was he going to be able to sort this out logically when his judgement was clouded by his desire for her? Even so, he couldn't stop himself asking, 'Ready for lunch?'

'I have one mum left to see.'

'Fine. Come and fetch me when you're free—I'll be in my office, wrestling with paperwork.' And wrestling with his need for her. Because his head knew this situation really wasn't fair to her.

And even though he lost himself in the paperwork, he was aware the second before Madison rapped on his open door.

'Do you need a couple of minutes to finish that?' she asked.

'I'm ready now,' he said, grabbing his jacket from the hook behind the door and shrugging it on. They bought sandwiches and a coffee to take out, then headed for the park. To Theo's surprise and pleasure, there was actually a bench free. 'Looks like we're in luck,' he said as they sat down. And even though he knew they ought to be discussing the situation between them, he didn't want the sunshine to go away just yet. He wanted just a couple of minutes when he could chat to her and pretend everything was fine, before they faced the tough questions. 'I noticed you were using sign language earlier. I had no idea anyone in the dcpartment knew it.'

'It can be useful if we have someone in who's deaf—a mum or their partner.'

'Like your mum today.'

She nodded.

'What made you learn sign language?' he asked.

'Guilt,' she said, surprising him.

'I don't understand.'

'Katrina has problems hearing—and it's my fault.' She toyed with her wrap. 'I gave her mumps when we were little.'

'Hey, that's not your fault at all. You know how quickly childhood illnesses sweep through schools and playgroups. She could have caught it from any other infected child, not just you.' He looked quizzically at her. 'So that was it? She had mumps and then afterwards everyone realised she couldn't hear properly?'

'Not quite. Kat was always a bit of a dreamer so if you called her and she didn't answer, you just assumed she'd gone into her own little world.' Madison shrugged. 'None of our family were medics. Our dads own a garage specialising in restoring ancient sports cars, Kat's mum's a PA and mine's a French teacher, so nobody gave it another thought—not until we were at university and I was doing a module on hearing loss.'

'And Kat fitted the profile?'

She nodded. 'You know how it is when you're a student. You spot symptoms everywhere—medical students have to be the worst hypochondriacs in the world! But eventually I convinced Kat to see her GP, who referred her to audiology and it seems she'd been unable to hear properly for years.' She shrugged. 'Kat couldn't really remember it being any different and just assumed that everyone else was like her. The hearing aid's made a huge difference and although she doesn't actually need to sign, she wanted to learn to do it in case any of her patients or their parents were deaf.'

'And you joined her in the classes.'

Madison smiled. 'I'm glad I did. We don't have many deaf mums but it's good to know I can help if they need me.' She looked straight at him. 'Kat can hear, but not brilliantly. She lip-reads quite a lot—and if you meet her and you patronise her, I'll murder you myself.'

He frowned. 'Why would I patronise her?'

'For being deaf.'

He stared at her, seeing the protectiveness on her face and appreciating that she looked out for her cousin, but completely mystified at the same time. 'I think I'm missing the point here.'

'If you're deaf,' Madison explained, 'and people know that, they do one of two things—either they shout, which isn't helpful, or they treat you as if you're slow and can't understand. That's absolutely not the case, but I guess you do miss things in a conversation—punchlines and banter and what have you—especially if people speak softly or cover their mouths when they talk or look away so you can't see their face, and…' She broke off with a grimace.

'What?'

'I was just thinking about Kat's ex. He was a complete and utter swine. I think he had low self-esteem, and the only way he could feel good about himself was to make her feel small. He used to make her feel useless, and treated her as if she was stupid—I mean, I know speaking slowly is helpful when someone's lip-reading you, but he took it to extremes. And she's not stupid. She's bright and funny and she doesn't expect special treatment. Her hearing is just part of her and he should've accepted that, not made a big thing about it.'

'Remind me never to upset you. You're scary when you're angry,' he said softly.

She grimaced. 'Sorry. It's just…'

'You love her, and it's instinctive to be protective of your family,' he said. 'I'm the same with my sisters. And my little brother—though as he's the same height as me now, he's made it clear I need to stop thinking of him as "little".'

She smiled ruefully. 'Thanks. For understanding.'

'I'm not an ogre, Maddie.'

'I know.' She paused. 'So what happens now, Theo?'

'I don't know. I hoped my subconscious was going to come up with something this morning,' he admitted, 'but it hasn't. I don't want to offer you anything less than you deserve, Maddie—but I don't know if I can give you what you want.'

'Marriage and babies.' She gave up the pretence of toying with her food. 'Theo, you don't panic about babies at work, do you?'

'No.' He knew what she was really asking. 'But that's because it's different. They're not my babies. I'm not in love with the mums. I can be calm and competent and reassure the mums in clinic or in a delivery room that everything's going to be fine. Whereas if you had my baby…my heart would be overruling my head, Maddie. I'd be an emotional mess. Panicking that I was going to lose you. And in a way what I do for a living makes it worse, because I know all the fine detail of everything that could possibly go wrong.' He blew out a breath. 'And that wouldn't be fair to you. You wouldn't be able to enjoy your pregnancy because you'd know how I was feeling, even if I tried to hide it.'

'And however much I reassured you, however much you knew intellectually that everything would be fine, there's the gap between head and heart. It's the same for me.'

He blinked. 'You're scared of being pregnant?'

'No. I'm scared of ending up in another marriage that's completely wrong for me,' she admitted. 'Last time, I was so sure. And I got it wrong. I can't trust my judgement. So even though I know you're an honourable man, Theo—that you'd never do what Harry did—the doubts still get in the way.'

He knew it wasn't tactful to ask, but he asked anyway. 'What happened with Harry?'

'It was my own fault.' She rolled her eyes. 'Kat told me not to marry him. She said she had a feeling he couldn't be trusted and she didn't want me to get hurt.'

'But you were in love with him and didn't listen?' he guessed.

She nodded. 'He swept me off my feet. We'd known each other all of three months when we got married.'

Three months? Lord. That was fast.

And he hadn't even known Madison that long.

So he had a feeling that this was going to be as much of an issue for her as it was for him. A relationship that was going way too fast. Maybe they needed to slow things down a bit.

'Looking back now, I can't believe how stupid I was,' she

continued. 'But at the time I thought we wanted the same things. A career and then children. Harry worked for a firm in the City. He wanted to be fast-tracked so he put in the hours, and I was working a junior doctor's usual mad hours, so we didn't get to see that much of each other—but it was great when he was with me.'

The flicker of jealousy shocked him. The man was clearly out of Madison's life, so why on earth should he be jealous? Especially given his fears about marriage and babies.

But this wasn't about him. It was about Madison. 'So was Kat right?' he asked softly.

'Yes.' She looked away. 'I came home early from work one day—I'd picked up a bug and I was feeling lousy. I didn't bother texting Harry to let him know I'd be home early because I didn't expect him to be there.' She shrugged. 'I just wanted to take some paracetamol, crawl into bed and go to sleep. I was on autopilot when I opened the door, didn't even notice a trail of clothing on the floor—and I walked in on them in our bedroom. My husband and his so-called colleague.'

Theo's fists clenched and he swore in Greek. 'How could he do that to you, Maddie?'

'I got my own back,' she said with a smile. 'I threw up all over her shoes. Designer shoes. Completely ruined them.'

But the smile didn't reach her eyes, and he could still see the flicker of hurt. Ruined shoes—no matter how expensive—didn't make up for a ruined marriage.

'Kat was brilliant. I texted her and she rang me and told me to go straight to her flat. She met me there and put me to bed and looked after me until I was over the bug. And she was there for me through the divorce. Just like I was there when Pete—her partner—decided to dump her for someone who wasn't, as he put it, "damaged goods".'

'He called her *what*?' Theo shook his head in disbelief.

'The way the men in your life have behaved, I'm surprised you're even talking to anyone male.'

Madison smiled. 'Not all men are bastards. Just as not all women are wonderful. People are who they are. Though I like to believe that people have a good heart, until proven otherwise.' She shrugged. 'So. Kat's waiting for her prince to come. I tried that for a while—but I discovered that Prince Charming was too damn lazy to find his way to me.'

'I'm not a prince,' he pointed out. 'And I hope I'm not charming.' In his opinion, charming usually meant shallow.

'You're charming,' she said, 'but it's more than skin deep with you.'

'Thank you for the compliment.' He inclined his head. 'So, does Katrina vet your men?'

She smiled. 'Sometimes.'

So maybe this was a way out without hurting her so much. Perhaps he should meet Katrina. Who, if she was as clear-sighted as Madison seemed to think, would see straight away that he was completely wrong for her cousin and talk sense into both of them. 'Maybe it's time we met.' His eyes held hers. 'I'd like to invite you both over to dinner. Talk to Kat, find out when she's free and give me some dates—oh, and let me know if there's anything she doesn't like foodwise.'

'You're going to cook for us?'

'Yes. And I'll make you crème brûlée for pudding.'

'You're on. Does this mean...?'

She stopped, but he could read the question in her eyes and it felt as if someone had just punched him. Hard. She was hoping that asking to meet her family was his way of saying he was serious about her. That he was going to give their future a chance.

Part of him wanted him to wrap his arms round her, hold her close, and tell her that she meant more to him than he'd ever expected anyone to do. That he was completely serious about her. That he wanted to let go of the fear and promise her everything she wanted…

But letting go was the hard part. And he wasn't sure he could do it. 'It means that my heart's overruling my head right now,' he said softly. 'I'm not promising anything, Maddie. Because I don't want to make you a promise I might not be able to keep.'

She reached over and squeezed his hand briefly. 'Thanks for being honest with me.'

'It doesn't feel as if I'm being honest,' he admitted. 'Even though I've told you things I've never spoken about with anyone else. I don't know if I can give you what you want, Maddie. And I don't know where we go from here. All I can suggest is that we…I don't know. See where this takes us.' He dragged in a breath. 'I want to offer you more. I really do. But I don't know if I can.'.

'That's honest. And I appreciate it.'

He couldn't bear to see the pain in her eyes. He looked away and took refuge in something safe. Work. 'We'd better get back to the ward before they send out a search party,' he said lightly.

'Yes. And I'll have a word with Sanjay and Nita about those scenarios you suggested.'

Back on safe ground, he thought with relief.

And somehow—*somehow*—he'd find a way to sort everything out. For both their sakes.

CHAPTER NINE

'YOU want me to sit in on your clinic?' Nita went pink with pleasure.

'Because I'm seeing some high-risk mums today and it'll be useful experience for you. I would've invited Sanjay along, too, had he not been off sick with a migraine,' Theo added, hoping that Nita would get the message. He was asking her along as a student, to give her experience with patients, not because he wanted her company in particular.

She was practically bubbling with happiness all the way down to the consultancy room. To his relief, she calmed down during the clinic and listened to the mums and asked intelligent questions.

Their final case that morning was a woman who'd been diagnosed with lupus before her pregnancy.

'What do you know about lupus?' he asked Nita.

'It's an autoimmune disease. It causes chronic inflammation in the skin, joints, blood and kidneys,' she recited, 'and it flares up in response to triggers, particularly stress. And it's a complication in pregnancy.'

'Absolutely correct. Good. Let's meet Mrs Hanson.'

Judith Hanson was all smiles as she walked in, and when Theo introduced Nita she immediately agreed to let the student sit in on their discussions.

'I see from your notes that you were diagnosed ten months ago, and your lupus was stable and in remission before you became pregnant,' Theo said.

She nodded. 'And I'm so pleased I was diagnosed—at least now I know why I had the three miscarriages.'

'Have you had a chance to talk to your family doctor or your rheumatologist?' Theo asked.

She nodded. 'And I've read up about it. I know there's a greater risk of the baby being stillborn if my kidneys are affected, and the baby might also grow slowly. The baby might have congenital heart problems—but the figures are one in a thousand, and I don't have the Rho antibodies that put my baby at greatest risk.'

'You're twelve weeks at the moment,' he said.

'Yes, and, touch wood, I haven't had a flare-up. I know that around forty per cent of women get worse, forty per cent stay as they are and twenty per cent go into complete remission during pregnancy.'

She really had done her research. Theo was impressed. 'There's also the possibility of a flare-up after the birth,' he said.

'Especially the second and eighth week after the birth—and it's most likely to affect my skin, joints and muscles.' She nodded. 'I'm going to get my mum to come and stay with me during those two weeks, just in case.'

'Sounds sensible.' But what amazed him most was that Mrs Hanson knew all the risks but had still been prepared to put herself through it for the sake of having a child. The same kind of bravery that Madison would show. The kind of bravery he somehow needed to learn. 'I'm impressed that you've read so much.'

'If you know what's going on, it takes most of the worry out and means the risks are calculated—you know where you are,' she said simply.

'So you probably already know I'll want to see you more often than my mums-to-be who don't have any complications,' he said. 'I'll also be talking to your rheumatologist and giving him regular updates. We'll be keeping an eye on your blood pressure—and I'm afraid I'll need extra blood tests, too.'

She nodded. 'I've got a list of the signs for pregnancy-induced hypertension—and I don't smoke or drink, I'm sensible about getting enough rest, and my diet is disgustingly healthy.'

He smiled. 'You know your stuff. Good.' He glanced through her notes. 'I'm happy with your blood pressure, there's no sign of any protein in your urine, and the blood-test results won't be back for a couple of days. I don't have any worries about you right now—but if you notice any changes in your condition or you have any worries at all, you'll come straight to me, yes?'

'Absolutely. I really want this baby, Mr Petrakis. When we lost our third baby, Frankie and I were devastated. But this little one's going to be just fine. I know it.' Mrs Hanson cradled her abdomen protectively.

'I should warn you,' he said gently, 'that you're less likely than the average mum to have a normal delivery. If you're ill or the baby's showing signs of distress, we'll need to do a section.'

She smiled. 'That's fine. I'm not taking any risks with the baby.'

'Or with yourself,' he added. 'Is there anything you'd like to ask me or Nita about?'

Mrs Hanson shook her head. 'Everything's fine. I'm not worried about anything.'

'Good. Would you mind if Nita examined you?'

'Not at all.' She hopped up onto the couch, lay back and allowed Nita to bare her abdomen and examine her.

He double-checked Nita's findings, confirmed them, and let her write them up in the notes; she turned pink with pleasure.

And then it was the end of his morning's clinic.

'You were brilliant,' Nita said.

He shrugged. 'No, Mrs Hanson was very well informed—and that's definitely something to encourage in our high-risk mums. The more they know, the more aware they are of any changes in their condition that aren't quite right, the better it will be because they'll come to us early enough for us to help effectively.'

'I still think you were brilliant.' She took a deep breath. 'Theo, you've been so good with me, helped me so much…I was wondering, um, can I take you out to dinner tonight?' The words came out in a rush.

Oh, lord. He really hadn't been expecting this. Even if he hadn't been involved with Madison, he wouldn't have accepted Nita's offer—but at the same time he wasn't going to be rude and obnoxious about it and make the girl feel embarrassed or hurt. 'It's very sweet of you to ask—thank you very much. But I'm afraid I already have plans for tonight.' Important plans. As in cooking dinner for Madison and her cousin.

'How about tomorrow?' she suggested.

She looked so full of hope and he felt horrible, stamping on her dreams like this, but he had to be honest to be kind. 'Nita, I'm very flattered that a clever and beautiful girl like you would ask me to dinner—particularly as I must be nearly fifteen years older than you are—but I'm sorry, I can't.'

She didn't say it, but it was written in her eyes. *Why?*

Well, he was going honest. May as well tell her the truth—just enough of it not to make life difficult for Madison. 'I'm seeing someone,' he explained.

'But…' She blinked. 'We never see you with anyone. Everyone thought you were single.'

He shrugged. 'My partner and I—' ha, what a way to describe Madison '—both hate gossip, so we keep it low key.'

'It sounds pretty serious.'

He nodded. It was. Which was why he was having such a hard time right now. He wanted her, and yet he couldn't give her what she wanted from life—so he ought to do the noble thing and end it, give her a chance to find someone who wanted the same things she wanted.

Nita looked embarrassed. 'I'm so sorry. I would never have asked you if I'd had any idea that you were involved with someone. I just…' Her voice faded.

Relief flooded through him. This wasn't going to be difficult, after all. 'It's not a problem, Nita. And it's not going to make any difference to the fact that we're colleagues. Come and have a coffee and you can tell me what you know about antiphospholipid syndrome and how to manage lupus in pregnancy—let's see how much you learned from Mrs Hanson.'

'Are you sure…? I mean, your gir—' She stopped abruptly. 'I mean, your partner…'

Remembering the way Madison had teased him on the very same subject, he chuckled. 'You were right first time. My partner's female. And she has coffee with colleagues all the time. It makes case conferences and teaching so much more civilised, don't you think?'

'Thank you. For being nice, when I've made a fool of myself.'

'You haven't made a fool of yourself,' he reassured her, and shepherded her down to the hospital café.

He only saw Madison in passing during the afternoon, and when he arrived home he was relieved that he'd suggested cooking dinner rather than going out somewhere. At least it meant he had something to do rather than just pace the house and wait for the time to pass until he met them. Something to do other than think about the fact that he really wanted Katrina to approve of him…and at the same time he really wanted her to disapprove of him, to tell Madison that he was completely wrong for her.

How could you want something so much and yet not want it at the same time?

He busied himself finishing the starters he'd begun making the previous evening, then took the pork from its marinade and began cooking the main course. Everything was bubbling away nicely when the doorbell rang, and Theo's heart skipped a beat.

He opened the door and Madison was there, smiling, holding a huge bunch of flowers.

Yet again she'd managed to surprise him.

'Flowers? For me?' he asked as she handed them to him.

'Not quite as spectacular as the ones you gave me the other day,' she said. Flowers that had made her eyes widen in delight. She smiled at him. 'I brought you some wine as well, but it's traditional to give your host flowers.'

He raised an eyebrow. 'Including male hosts?'

Her eyes were filled with amusement. 'Don't be so sexist, *Kyrios* Petrakis.'

'*Signomi*, Madison. I should remember my manners and thank you properly.' He swept into a low bow. 'I deeply honoured by your gift, *Despinida* Madison,' he said, making the English words sound heavily accented. 'Please to come into house and sit down.' Enjoying himself, he hammed it up even more. 'I with you soon. I check dinner. Me no want burn food like *Despinida* Madison does.'

Madison cuffed his arm. 'Behave, Theo.'

'You started it,' he reminded her with a grin, then turned to the woman beside her. 'Hello, Katrina. Pleased to meet you, and I apologise for my poor manners. Do come in.'

He ushered them through into the living room, where Madison handed him a bottle of red wine and a bottle of white. 'I wasn't sure what you were cooking, so I erred on the side of caution.'

'*Efkharisto, matia mou.*' He kissed her lightly on the cheek.

Katrina gave him a box of dark chocolates. 'Maddie tells me you like these ones.'

He smiled at her. 'I do indeed. Thank you very much—they'll be perfect with coffee.' He wrinkled his nose. 'I have to admit, that's the one thing I forgot to buy. Which, considering that this evening involves dinner and Madison, was incredibly stupid of me.'

'Coffee. Uh-oh. Please, tell me you're not going to make us Greek coffee?' Madison asked, looking appalled.

'*Kardoula mou*, I told you I was making you a traditional Greek meal,' he reminded her.

She groaned. 'So we get gloopy coffee. And Greek meals don't include chocolate.'

He laughed. 'Of course they do. The cocoa tree is *theobroma cacao*, and "theobroma" is Greek for "food of the gods".' He smiled. 'But I'll stop teasing you and admit it's not a completely traditional Greek meal, because I know someone who would live on a certain French pudding and Italian coffee if she could.'

Madison's face brightened. 'You bought crème brûlée?'

'No.' He hadn't bought it. He'd made it for her himself, the previous evening. From scratch. With a bit of telephone help from his sister Melina. But he wasn't going to tell her that just yet. 'Can I get you both a glass of wine? White or red?'

'White, please,' Katrina said.

'Same for me, please,' Madison said. 'Can I do anything to help?'

'You, *hara mou*, helping in a kitchen? Willingly? Hmm, now, that's a new one,' he teased.

Katrina laughed. 'He clearly knows you well, Maddie.'

Madison smiled ruefully. 'I don't mind washing up.'

'This evening,' Theo said, 'you're here as my guest. So, no, you're not washing up tonight. But thank you for the offer.'

He went into the kitchen, took a bottle of white wine from the fridge and filled two glasses for Madison and Katrina, then switched the steamer on.

'Ten minutes until dinner,' he said, returning to the living room with the wine.

'I'm afraid I've been very nosy about your photographs,' Katrina said, gesturing to the pictures on the mantelpiece.

'My family.' He went through them, putting names to the faces for her. 'There are more in the dining room.'

'I can't imagine what it was like, growing up as one of five,' Katrina said.

'Noisy,' Theo said. 'And a lot of fun.'

'You must miss them horribly.'

'I do.' He wrinkled his nose. 'I know we have IM and webcams as well as the phone, but it's not the same as being there with them. And every time I see my niece and nephew, they've changed so much.'

'So are you going back to Greece when your secondment's over?'

He knew exactly what Katrina was asking: *Are you going to break Maddie's heart?*

'Right now,' he said quietly, 'I really don't know. I'll go back soon because it's been six weeks since I've seen them, and that's too long.'

'So you're taking a week's holiday?' Madison asked.

Theo shrugged. 'A long weekend, perhaps.' And although part of him wanted to ask her to go with him, he knew it would be a mistake. It would raise too many expectations—with Madison herself, as well as with his family.

They'd absolutely adore her.

And press him to set a date for the wedding.

Except he wasn't quite ready for that. He still had things he needed to sort out in his head. So did Madison. It was best to leave things as they were.

He glanced at his watch. 'Would you like to come through into the dining room?' He ushered them through, then turned to Katrina. 'I apologise in advance if I'm being patronising—that's really not my intention—but Maddie tells me you have some hearing loss. I've tried to set the table so you can see both our faces, to make it easier for you to lip-read, but if I've got it wrong please feel free to move things around.'

Katrina smiled. 'It looks absolutely fine. Thank you—and you're not being patronising, you're being thoughtful.'

Madison glanced at the table. 'Wow. That's dinner?'

'It's the first course. *Mezedes*,' he explained. As Katrina and Madison sat down, he talked them through the dishes: taramasalata, tzatziki—yoghurt with chopped cucumber and mint—tiny triangles of feta and spinach wrapped in filo pastry known as *spanikopita*, stuffed vine leaves and plenty of wholegrain bread.

'Maddie said you were a great cook,' Katrina said when she'd tasted a bit of everything. 'I see what she means. These pastries are fabulous.'

He inclined his head. '*Efkharisto*.'

She was even more enthusiastic about the main course, a rich Greek stew which Theo served with fluffy rice and steamed vegetables.

'It's *afelia*—well, our family's version of the recipe,' he said with a smile. 'My sister Melina is a chef. I borrowed this one from her.'

'Obviously it includes pork, red wine…and ground coriander?' Katrina hazarded.

'Yes.' He was impressed that she'd picked out the ingredients so easily. 'And a cinnamon stick in the marinade.'

'It's gorgeous. Trade you the recipe for this for my recipe for lasagne?'

'She makes the best lasagne in the world—better even than my mum,' Madison added.

'Sounds good to me. It's a deal, Katrina.' He glanced at Madison, then back at Katrina. 'Your cousin told me that you were the cook and she'd rather do the ironing.'

Katrina smiled. 'Which suits me fine, because I *loathe* ironing.'

'So you always wanted to be a doctor?' he asked.

'I suppose I was following in Maddie's footsteps,' Katrina admitted. 'Though if I hadn't been a doctor, I would probably have been a chef.'

'Half the time she believes that fixing people involves feeding them,' Madison added.

'Half the time, it does,' Katrina said. 'You think how many stress-related illnesses there are. If people took a little more time, ate together and communicated properly…they'd be under a lot less strain and their health would be better.'

'That,' Theo said, 'is a very fair point. Though some people find it hard to communicate.' And some things were incredibly difficult to talk about. Like the things he knew he should tell Madison, but he didn't know where to start.

'Communication problems is where food really comes into its own,' Katrina said.

'Preferably pudding,' Madison added with a grin.

'Eat your main course, *kardoula mou*, and you can have pudding,' Theo said.

'And this was the man who once promised to cook me an entire dinner of puddings,' Madison grumbled teasingly.

Though when Theo cleared the plates away and brought through a platter of fresh fruit, her face fell.

'This is your idea of a non-Greek, international pudding?'

'Isn't it yours?'

'Hmm.'

He smiled. '*Matia mou*, were you hoping I'd made something French?'

'No-o.'

It was a very obvious fib, and he ruffled her hair. 'One moment.' He disappeared to the kitchen, returned with a shallow dish containing the crème brûlée and a blowtorch, and proceeded to caramelise the sugar there and then at the table.

'That's just showing off,' Maddie said, folding her arms. 'Big time.'

He spread his hands. 'Insult the cook, *kardia mou*, and you don't get pudding.'

'I take it back,' she said quickly, then tipped her head to one side and looked at him. 'You actually made this for me?'

He rolled his eyes. 'Did you think I'd bought it from a deli and just added a bit of sugar and the blowtorch to impress you?'

'Take pity on the girl. She hates cooking,' Katrina reminded him.

Theo brushed the backs of his fingers against Madison's cheek. 'I rang Melina last night and got a few tips on how to make crème brûlée. And, yes, *hara mou*, I made it especially for you.'

Pudding was followed by coffee—lattes for Madison and Katrina and strong black coffee for Theo—and chocolates. They were so busy talking and laughing that the time simply vanished—and with a start Madison realised it was gone eleven p.m. 'We'd better be going—we're both on early shift tomorrow,' she said.

'I'd drive you myself had I not had that second glass of wine. So I'll call you a taxi,' Theo said immediately.

'Theo, we're one stop away on the tube,' Madison protested. 'And there are two of us. We live three doors away from each other.'

'I don't care. At this time of night, you're taking a taxi,' he insisted. 'And I'm paying. No arguments.'

Theo was implacable so, in the end Madison submitted with good grace. When the taxi arrived, he kissed Katrina's cheek and then Madison's, and she suppressed a pang of disappointment that he hadn't kissed her goodbye properly. Or maybe, she thought, he hadn't wanted to appear too pushy in front of Katrina.

'He's the one, isn't he?' Katrina asked as the taxi pulled away.

'What do you mean?' Madison asked.

'Gorgeous mind, gorgeous heart—and very easy on the eye.' Katrina smiled. 'And he's a fantastic cook. He ticks every single box on your list, Maddie.'

'Did you likc him?'

Katrina nodded. 'He's a nice guy. I liked the fact his mantelpiece was full of family photographs—and I noticed he has children's drawings on his fridge, held there with magnets.'

'They're his niece's.'

'That's the only thing. Do you think he'll change his mind about the issue of kids?'

'I don't know.'

'So where do you go from here?'

'I have no idea.' Madison sighed. 'I don't even know how he really feels about me.'

'I think I do,' Katrina said thoughtfully. 'Did you realise he watches you all the time?'

Madison frowned. 'What do you mean, he watches me?'

'He looks at you as if you're the focal point in a room—

and there's a special softness in his eyes when he looks at you. When he smiles at you, it's not the same way he smiles at anyone else. There's a lot more depth to it. And he calls you "darling" all the time.'

'No, he doesn't.'

'He does,' Katrina insisted. 'Well, strictly speaking, "*matia mou*" means "my eyes", but in Greek that's a really romantic thing to call someone.'

Madison gave her cousin a curious look. 'How come you know so much about Greek endearments?'

Katrina coughed. 'Someone I met on holiday. Years ago. And it wasn't serious and it didn't go further than a kiss and holding hands, so don't give me a grilling. Besides, we're talking about you and Theo. He loves you, Maddie. And every time he looks at you, he looks torn. As if he doesn't want to love you, but he can't help himself.' She paused. 'And you look that way at him, too.'

Madison knew that her cousin noticed more than most people; Katrina had grown used to picking up visual cues to compensate for her poor hearing. And Katrina was also a stickler for the truth. 'It scares me, Kat. The way I feel about him. It's even stronger than the way I felt about Harry. And suppose I've got it just as wrong this time?'

'Somehow, I don't think you have.' Katrina took Madison's hand and squeezed it. 'I'd say hang on in there, hon. Because when Theo's sorted out whatever the problem is in his head, he'll be worth the wait.'

CHAPTER TEN

'I LIKE Katrina very much,' Theo informed Madison over lunch the following day. 'I can certainly see the family resemblance.' The corners of his eyes crinkled. 'She's lovely—though my taste runs to smaller, livelier baggages.'

Madison blinked. 'Did you just call me a baggage?'

'I might've done.' He leaned back in his chair and smiled at her. 'What are you going to do about it?'

'Make you take it back.'

His smile widened. 'And how exactly are you going to do that, Madison Gregory—given that I'm so much bigger than you are?'

'I'm coming home with you after work. And when I've eaten the rest of that fabulous crème brûlée you made—which, by the way, you'd better not have eaten for breakfast this morning…'

Theo burst out laughing. 'Maddie, only you would eat pudding for breakfast.'

'Don't knock it until you've tried it. Kat's chocolate bread-and-butter pudding is even better cold—though that's reserved as a birthday breakfast treat. Anyway, stop distracting me. As I said, when I've finished the crème brûlée…then I'll show you.'

He raised an eyebrow. 'That sounds more like a promise than a threat.'

'It is.' She smiled. 'I didn't say that it wasn't going to be enjoyable, did I?'

He laughed. 'In that case maybe I should insult you more often, *matia mou*.'

'Hmm.' She looked at him through lowered lashes. Kat was right: there was a softness in his eyes when he looked at her. So maybe he did love her. But she needed to hear the words for herself. From him.

'Actually, I have a better idea than the crème brûlée,' he said. 'I discovered that the jazz trio who played at the masked ball happens to be playing at a club in Soho tonight. Let's go dancing.'

They hadn't been dancing since the night they'd first met. And the idea of dancing cheek to cheek again with Theo, to her favourite kind of music… 'I'd love to.'

'Good.' He gave her that warm smile. 'And, Maddie?'

'Yes?'

'Take a taxi from your place to mine,' he said softly. 'And if you want to bring an overnight bag with you…'

Her heart missed a beat. 'Is that what you want?'

'Yes. Though I still can't make you any promises,' he warned.

'Understood.' Though he was definitely letting her closer. Maybe, just maybe, this was going to work out.

Madison was still on cloud nine when she had her first case of the afternoon.

'I don't mind your student being here at all,' Mrs Reeves said when Madison asked her permission for Nita to sit in on the appointment. 'I don't care who I see, if you can make this itching stop!'

'Where's the itching?' Madison asked.

'My hands, the soles of my feet, my arms and my legs.' Mrs Reeves started rubbing her arms. 'Sorry. It's driving me crazy.'

'Try not to scratch, or you'll make it even more sore,'

Madison said gently. 'You might find pressing your skin helps, or putting something cool against your skin.'

The symptoms were absolutely classic, so she let Nita take the lead, eliciting Mrs Reeves's medical history, doing a blood-pressure check, palpating the baby and checking for the baby's heartbeat.

'It's keeping me awake,' Mrs Reeves said. 'It's a lot worse at night. I've been to see my doctor twice—but he says there isn't a rash and there's no obvious reason for it.'

Apart from obstetric cholestasis, Madison thought.

'Does anyone in your family have eczema, asthma or allergies?' Nita asked.

Mrs Reeves shook her head.

Nita glanced at Madison. 'I think I need to do a blood test.'

'My GP's already done that, a month ago,' Mrs Reeves said. 'It was normal.'

'Sometimes,' Madison said, 'it takes more than one test before we see anything show up in the results. Even if this one's clear, I'd want to do a test in two weeks' time if you're still itching.'

'So do you know what it is?'

'It's called obstetric cholestasis,' Nita said, her voice becoming more confident at Madison's nod. 'It's a problem of the liver you get during pregnancy—and it's caused by pregnancy hormones, so the itching will stop after your baby's born.'

'Heaven help me if this one's late,' Mrs Reeves said in dismay. 'I'm only thirty-four weeks—I can't stand the idea of another two months or so of this!'

'Hopefully it won't come to that. I'd like to take a blood test,' Nita said. 'The oestrogen produced by your body affects the way your liver deals with bile salts, which build up in your blood and cause the itching.'

'What if the test doesn't show a thing?'

'Then we can look at ways of calming the itch for you,' Nita said. 'May I take a blood sample?'

Mrs Reeves nodded. 'I used to be scared of needles. But the amount I've had stuck in me during pregnancy…'

'It does get better,' Nita reassured her.

When she'd taken the sample under Madison's supervision, Madison mouthed, 'Urine sample.'

Nita handed Mrs Reeves a small clear bottle. 'Can you do me a mid-stream urine sample too, please?'

'Sure. When will the blood test results be back?'

Nita glanced at Madison.

'This afternoon,' Madison said. 'If you don't mind waiting around a bit, I can slot you back in at the end of my list today.'

'If that means you can get the itching to stop, I'd be happy to wait until midnight,' Mrs Reeves said with feeling.

'You probably already know that the café's on the next floor up,' Madison said. 'Come back in about three hours, and bring your sample with you.'

'Will do.'

Roughly halfway through the list, Madison took a five-minute comfort break. And when she came back, she squeezed Nita's hand. 'Before we see the rest of our list, I wanted a word. You're doing really, really well here. But you've been a bit quiet since yesterday. Are you worried about anything?'

'No, I'm fine.'

'No, you're not,' Madison said gently. 'Would it help to talk?'

'Not really.' Nita wrinkled her noise. 'It's just that I made a real idiot of myself yesterday.'

'How?' Madison asked.

Nita sighed. 'I know that it's not really done for people to go out together on the same ward, especially students with senior doctors, but as this is the last week of my rotation, I thought maybe…' She sighed again. 'I can't believe I was that stupid. Of course a man that gorgeous was going to be attached.'

'Theo?' She'd thought for a while that Nita had a crush on the consultant. But Nita had said the man she'd asked out was attached. Would Theo have told anyone that he was seeing *her*?

'Theo,' Nita confirmed. 'It took me a week to get my nerve up to ask him. He was really nice about it—and I think that's made it worse.' She looked miserable. 'He just said that he was really flattered but, sorry, he was already involved with someone. He said they kept it low key but it was really serious.'

Theo had told someone that he was really serious about her? Did this mean he was really thinking about a future with her? Or had he just tried to be kind and let Nita down gently?

He certainly couldn't have told Nita who he was seeing, or the student would never have confided in her.

'Never mind,' she said reassuringly. 'I'm sure there won't be any awkwardness between you in this last week of your attachment, because you're both too professional to let that happen.' She hugged Nita swiftly. 'Don't take it to heart. You're not the first who's said something they wished they could take back, and you won't be the last. You weren't to know he was already seeing someone.'

'I suppose not. I wonder who it is?' Nita looked speculative. 'His face went all soft and dreamy when he talked about her.'

Exactly what Katrina had said.

Madison's heart missed another beat and she really hoped that she didn't look equally dreamy when Theo's name was mentioned. Because, if she did, before too long someone would notice and make the connection. And neither of them was ready to go public. Not until the stalemate was broken.

'Well, we'd better get back to our list,' Madison said with a smile.

At the end of the day, they saw Mrs Reeves again.

'We've had the blood results back,' Madison said. 'And it's pretty conclusive.' She looked at the dark urine sample. 'Can I ask you, are you drinking plenty?'

'Drinking lots and weeing lots,' Mrs Reeves said wryly.

'Dark urine is another sign,' Madison explained. 'I know this is driving you crazy, and the only real cure for the condition is to give birth—so I'm going to induce you at thirty-seven weeks.'

'Is the baby all right?' Mrs Reeves asked, looking worried.

'Yes. There's no scientific evidence to say that your condition will affect your baby's growth or development,' Madison reassured her. 'Though obviously it's uncomfortable for you.'

'You can say that again.' Mrs Reeves scratched the palms of her hands. 'So I just have to put up with this itching for another three weeks?'

'Yes, but I should warn you it might last for another three weeks after the baby's born and your hormones have settled down again.'

'I think I'm going to go mad,' Mrs Reeves said softly. 'Isn't there anything at all you can give me?'

'I know it's horrible for you. There is a drug that can reduce the bile salts in your blood,' Madison said, 'but it's not licensed for use in pregnancy and I don't know of any trials we can piggy-back. What I can do is give you a prescription for some cream that will help. And then there are the obvious self-help things like wearing cotton clothing, bathing your skin with cool water and trying to press rather than scratch your skin—the last thing you need on top of the itching is an infection because scratching has broken your skin and some bacteria have taken advantage.'

'It might also be worth trying classes to help you relax, like yoga,' Nita suggested. 'Stress can make itching worse and relaxation can make it a bit better.'

'I'm also going to prescribe some vitamin K for you, because this condition means your body can't absorb the vitamin as well as it normally would from your diet,' Madison said. 'You'll need to take the powder in water every day.'

'What does vitamin K do?' Mrs Reeve asked.

'If you have enough vitamin K, you're at less risk of bleeding heavily after the baby's born. The baby will also need an injection of vitamin K at birth, but that's routine for all babies—absolutely nothing to worry about,' Madison reassured her.

'And then the itching will go?'

Madison nodded. 'Though, as I said, it can take up to three weeks after the birth. You'll also need to have some blood tests a couple of weeks after the birth to check your liver function and make sure everything's normal again. Do you normally use the contraceptive Pill?'

'Yes.'

'As long as the itching has cleared up, you should be able to use it again—but if you start itching when you go back on the Pill, you'll need to see your GP and maybe try a different form of contraceptive.' Madison smiled at her. 'Is there anything else you'd like to ask us, or anything you'd like me to run through again?'

'No. I think I know what to expect now. And thanks. This itching's been driving me crazy.'

Mmm, Maddie knew all about being driven crazy. But she'd take Katrina's advice and wait until Theo was ready to let her close.

That evening, Madison took a taxi to Theo's, as agreed.

'You look stunning,' he said when he opened the door to her and kissed her hello. 'Forget the crème brûlée. I'm going to take you out to dinner before we go to the jazz club.'

Dinner, in a little bistro, was fabulous. Theo was at his most charming and talkative and Madison enjoyed his company hugely. But he didn't say a word about his encounter with Nita—and Madison didn't want to be the one to bring it up.

The jazz club was even better. Dancing with Theo to the kind of music she loved, holding him close. And then back to his house, where he undressed her in silence, caressing every inch of skin with his hands and his mouth as he uncovered it before making such sweet and tender love with her that she was close to tears.

'Maddie,' he said softly, holding her close. 'There's something I need to tell you.'

For one mad moment she thought he was really going to say it.

I love you.

She was prepared to tell him that she loved him, too—all the way back.

But his next words sent ice through her veins.

'You know what we were saying last night? About me missing home?'

Oh, no. Please, don't say he was leaving. There were still weeks to go before his locum consultancy ended—weren't there? Surely they still had time to get to know each other, work through their fears and face the future together?

'I'm going back for a few days the day after tomorrow.'

'Sure.' What did he expect her to say? Anticipation prickled up her spine. Or was he going to ask her to go with him, meet his family? It was a bit late notice, but she could probably get someone to swap shifts with her.

'I'll send you a postcard,' he said lightly.

Oh. So he *wasn't* going to ask her to go with him.

She suppressed the little sting of hurt. Although he'd seemed different over the last few days, as if he was falling for her, she'd been a fool to hope for anything more.

'That'd be nice,' she said, hoping that she sounded equally light and unconcerned.

And although Theo curled his body round hers that night, holding her close, she found it hard to fall asleep that night. She faked deep and regular breathing, but it wasn't enough to tip her over the edge into sleep. She lay awake, listening to Theo's breath and the ticking of the clock. Katrina had said he'd be worth the wait once he'd sorted out the problems in his head. But would he ever let her close enough to help him sort them out?

Three days later, Theo emerged from the sea, slicking his wet hair back from his forehead. Lord, it felt good to be home. And a hard swim in the sea was exactly what he'd needed.

He walked across the beach and sat down on the towel next to Sophronia.

'Better now?' his sister asked.

'I don't know what you're talking about.'

'Yes, you do.' She checked that the sunshade was still in the right place to give maximum cover to her sleeping toddler, then drew her knees up to her chin. 'What's her name?'

'Whose name?'

'The woman you've been brooding about since—well, probably since the moment you got on the plane yesterday. And don't deny it, Theo.'

'Because women have a sixth sense about these things?' he asked lightly.

'Because you rang Meli to ask for tips on a special pudding. Which means you were cooking for someone.'

Oh, lord. He'd forgotten about the family grapevine. He'd bet his sisters had been speculating ever since.

'So be as snippy as you like, *adelphos mou*,' she said sweetly. 'You're still going to tell me.'

'There's nothing to tell, Sophie.'

She pulled her sunglasses down her nose just enough for him to see her eyes and stared at him. 'Theo, it isn't a weakness to talk to people about emotional things, you know. And bottling things up isn't good for you.'

'I don't—' he began.

She held up a hand and made the kind of noise parents made to tell their children to stop talking right that second.

It worked. He shut up.

'Theo, you *know* you bottle things up. You're like all the other men in our family—you think that being strong and silent is a good thing. I'm telling you, it isn't. So either you talk to me, *adelphos mou*, or I'll nag you stupid until you go back to England.'

He knew from past experience that his sister was perfectly capable of carrying out her threat.

'Your choice,' she finished, folding her arms.

He sighed. 'All right. Her name is Madison. Maddie, for short.'

'And?'

'She works with me. She's a registrar.'

Sophronia nodded and pushed her sunglasses back up to their normal place. 'Good. She understands your work and you have things in common. So what's the problem?'

'There isn't a problem.'

'Then why didn't you bring her home to meet us? Are you scared we won't like her?'

'You'd all love her,' Theo admitted. 'She's bright and lively and good to have around.' And he missed her—shockingly, to the point where it was like a physical pain. He ached for her to be there, next to him. 'She orders her meals backwards—pudding first; she likes dancing to old-fashioned music; and she spends her spare time organising fundraisers for the hospital.'

'So she's fun and has a good heart. Exactly the kind of woman I'd want for my brother. Then what's the problem?' Sophronia asked again.

It was a long, long time before he answered. 'I'm the problem.'

'How?'

He sighed. 'I suppose I'm scared.'

'Scared?' She raised an eyebrow. 'My big brother, who's not scared of anything and who's always told me to forget about the spiders and reach for the stars—and Meli, Thali and Stefanos too—scared?'

Theo waved a dismissive hand. 'This is different.'

'How?'

'It's a risk. Putting your heart in someone else's hands.'

'Yes,' Sophronia agreed. 'But it's a risk worth taking, in my considered opinion. Theo, to know you is to love you, and you've had women dropping at your feet for years.' She frowned. 'Or is that it? She's unavailable?'

Theo smiled wryly. 'No. She was married—but it ended a long time ago. *Not* her fault,' he added firmly.

'Does your Maddie know how you feel about her? Have you told her?'

'Yes and no. She knows why I've avoided marriage and babies.'

'You told her about your mother?' Sophronia blinked hard.

He shrugged. 'I wanted to be honest with her.'

'Hmm. Do you know how she feels about you?'

He shrugged. 'I guess she likes me.'

'Theo.' She cuffed his arm. 'You know what I mean. If you love someone and they love you back—if they're The One, you *know*. Just like when I met Andreas. I knew the second I met him.'

Just as Theo had known, the second he'd seen Madison.

'She's The One,' Theo said softly, 'and it makes me freeze in panic.'

'It sounds to me as if you're in love. *Really* in love. For the first time. Yes, it's scary.'

Yes. But it wasn't the real problem. Theo took a deep breath. He also knew why he'd come home. Why he'd sought out the oldest of his siblings for a quiet chat on the beach. Because he knew he needed to get this sorted out in his head, and he had no idea where to start. And his sister was very, very good at sorting things out. 'I'm scared of losing her, Sophie,' he said quietly. 'What if it goes wrong, the same way it did for my mother?'

Sophronia glanced around, as if to double-check everyone was out of earshot, and lowered her voice. 'What happened to your mother wasn't your fault, Theo.'

Strictly speaking, Theo thought, it was.

'And it wasn't Dad's either. It was a tragedy, desperately sad, but it happened and you can't do anything to change the past.' She took his hand and squeezed it. 'I'm sorry you didn't get the chance to know her. But you do still have a mother. Mine—and she thinks of herself as your mother. We *all* think of her that way.'

'I know. Me, too. Eleni's been my mother since I was four.' He sighed. 'Sophie, don't say anything to Dad or Eleni about this, will you? I'd hate them to think I…' His throat seemed to close.

She nodded. 'They know you love them, *agapi mou*. And I know it's a difficult subject for Dad—like you, he bottles things up. But, you know, they would hate to think that you still carry so much pain around with you.' She stroked his forehead. 'They want you to be happy. That's why they keep pushing eligible women your way. I know you think it's all to do with business and dynasties, but it's not that at all. They want you to be as happy as they are. Settled, at the centre of your family.'

'It drives me crazy.'

'I know.' She smiled. 'I've told them you're big enough and ugly enough to choose your own partner.'

'I've found her. But…' He shook his head in frustration. 'Maddie wants children.'

'And so do you. Look at the way you are with Arianna, telling her stories and letting her beat you in swimming races and building sandcastles for her. Look at how you are with Petros, cuddling him and singing him songs. You'll make a fantastic dad.' She paused, and pushed her sunglasses up over her hair so she could look straight at him. 'Theo, you're an obstetric consultant. How often does the kind of complication your mother had happen?'

'Rarely,' he admitted. 'But it still happens.'

'But you said the key word, *adelphos mou*. It's *rare*. And there's no reason why it would happen to Maddie.' She sighed. 'Theo, you have to let it go. Leave the past where it is and look to the future. And you have to take your courage in both hands and face that risk—for both your sakes. If she loves you and you've been blowing hot and cold on her, she must be going crazy.'

'I know. And I don't mean to blow hot and cold on her. I just…'

'You think you're doing her a favour by pushing her away?' Sophronia rolled her eyes. 'Men! Theo, that's not how it works. Trust me. If she loves you, you're breaking her heart. So *tell* her—tell her what you told me. If she's the woman who deserves you, she'll understand. And she'll be the one to make your heart whole again.'

He knew his sister was right. Though it was easier said than done. If anything happened to Madison—if he lost her, the way his father had lost his mother—he'd never be able to forgive himself.

'I believe in you, *agapi mou*,' Sophronia said softly. 'Go back to England. Tell your Maddie how you feel about her. And if Arianna isn't a flower girl by the end of the year, you are in *so* much trouble,' she added with a grin.

Theo smiled back. 'Noted. And, Sophie?'

She tipped her head on one side. 'Yes?'

'Thanks.' He hugged her. 'I think that's why I came home.'

'To get advice on your love life from your little sister?' she teased.

'Sometimes,' he said wryly, 'I think you're wiser than I am.'

'Of course I am. You know as well as I do that "sophie" means "wisdom".' She ruffled his still-damp hair. 'And I'm female, which gives me an extra advantage over you anyway.'

'I think,' he said ruefully, 'Maddie is going to adore you. And you're going to gang up on me.'

She smiled. 'Because we will have your best interests at heart, *adelphos mou*. Go back to England, Theo. That's where your heart is.'

'What, you're chucking me out already?'

She rolled her eyes. 'You know you can stay as long as you like. We'll always have room for you, Theo. But I think you will be happier if you go back to England. Sort things out with Maddie. And next time you come make sure you bring her with you.'

'I wouldn't dare do otherwise,' he said.

CHAPTER ELEVEN

MADISON was feeling seriously out of sorts. And it wasn't just because she was missing Theo. For goodness' sake, he'd been away all of a day and a half, and she was well past the teenager stage of counting the seconds since they'd last seen each other. He'd sent her a text to let her know he'd arrived safely, and a picture of the sunset the previous evening. It wasn't as if he was ignoring her.

But she still felt odd. Her breasts were sore—which she assumed meant that her period was about to start, and accounted for the fit of the grumps too. But she also found herself going to the loo more often that day. And at lunchtime the scent of coffee in the cafeteria made her feel slightly queasy.

Clearly she'd eaten something that disagreed with her, because she couldn't face eating anything other than a cheese sandwich and some fruit, and there was an odd metallic taste in her mouth.

If she hadn't known better, she'd think she was having the same symptoms their mums-to-be described to her or the midwives at their first antenatal appointment.

Crazy. Of course not.

But the idea was insidious. It stayed in her head all day;

and although she managed to push it aside during ward rounds and clinic, it nudged itself to the forefront while she was doing her paperwork.

Could she be pregnant?

Surely not. She and Theo had been careful to take precautions.

But his words flickered into her head: *No matter how careful we are with contraception, you know as well as I do that the only one hundred per cent guaranteed contraception is abstinence.*

She shook herself. This was crazy. How many couples had she seen at clinic who'd confided to her how long it had taken them to get pregnant—months and months of trying and timing their love-making for the tiny window of ovulation each month? So even if the condom had failed, how likely was it that she'd be pregnant?

Then again, it only took one sperm to fertilise an egg.

And the couples she'd talked to were in their mid-thirties. Older than her, with their fertility rate dropping.

She counted back rapidly in her head. Oh, lord. Her cycle wasn't brilliantly regular; sometimes her period arrived three or four days early and sometimes it arrived three or four days late, so she hadn't given it a second thought that her period was a bit late.

Maybe it was going to be even later this month.

But all the same, on her way home from work she went to a supermarket she didn't usually use and bought a pregnancy test. She didn't bother reading the packaging—after all these years as a doctor specialising in maternity care, she knew exactly how they worked—and did the test.

One blue line: good, the test was working.

And now the other box would be clear and she could stop being so paranoid.

Except, as she watched, it wasn't clear.

There was a second blue line. Fainter than the other, but still there.

Positive.

So she was pregnant.

Oh, help.

This pregnancy wasn't planned. Wasn't expected.

And although part of her was delighted—she'd be proud to have Theo's baby—she knew he was going to react badly. Given what he'd told her about his past, her pregnancy would be his worst nightmare come true.

Worse, he might think she'd done it on purpose. To force the issue. Break the stalemate they'd had before he'd gone to Greece.

She only hoped that he'd believe she was telling him the truth.

Telling him.

Somehow she was going to have to find the right words. To reassure him that what had happened to his mother wasn't going to happen to her.

She curved a protective hand over her abdomen, then smiled wryly at herself. Right now she was officially five weeks pregnant, counting back to the first day of her last period. It'd be another week until the baby was officially a foetus, when the spine and nervous system started to form and it would be the size of a baked bean. And another six weeks after that until the threat of a miscarriage was reduced.

It was still early days. Really early days.

But she wasn't going to lie to him. As soon as he came back from Greece, she'd tell him.

She had a long, warm bath—not too hot, for the baby's sake—and had just settled back against her pillows, trying to think about how she was going to broach the subject to Theo, when her mobile phone rang.

The screen told her it was Theo.

'*Kalispera*, Maddie. How are you?' he asked.

Pregnant. Worried. Out of sorts. 'Fine,' she fibbed. 'I wasn't expecting you to ring me.'

'No? Hmm. I haven't behaved very well to you, *matia mou*. I'm sorry. I just…' He sighed. 'You know the situation. And my sister Sophronia says I am like all men—I never talk about the important stuff.'

Uh-oh. This didn't sound good. 'Such as?'

'The phone isn't the place to discuss it, *kardoula mou*. But I'll be home the day after tomorrow. We'll talk then.'

'Should I be worried?' she asked, striving to keep her tone light.

'No. But I'm going to be home long before a postcard would reach you. I'll bring you back something instead.'

'Theo, I'm not expecting a present. Really. You're supposed to be spending time with your family.'

'I am. And it's good to be home.' He paused. 'Are you OK? You sound a bit…'

'I'm just a bit tired,' she said swiftly.

'OK. Can I take you out to dinner when I'm back?'

Given how sick she'd felt in the cafeteria earlier that day, going somewhere that involved cooking smells might not be a good idea. But she could hardly say that without explaining why—and she needed to discuss this face to face, not over the phone. 'That'd be lovely,' she fibbed.

'Good. My flight gets in at four. Give me time to collect my luggage, get through customs and catch the train back from the airport… I'll call for you at seven.'

'OK.' And by then she would've worked out how to tell him the news. 'I'll see you the day after tomorrow.'

'The day after tomorrow,' he repeated. 'And, Maddie?'

'Yes?'

'I…' He stopped, and said, 'Sleep well.'

'You, too.' Though she didn't think she would somehow.

* * *

Lord, he missed her so much, Theo thought. But now he had everything sorted out in his head. He trusted Madison. So tonight he'd talk to her and explain why he'd kept her at a distance. He just had to hope she'd understand why he hadn't been able to bring himself to discuss it before—and then he'd produce the small velvet-covered box currently sitting in his pocket. He'd ask her to marry him. And then, with her by his side, maybe the fear would go away and he could get on doing what he wanted to do for the rest of his life.

Loving her.

He rang the doorbell to the flat and waited; rather than buzzing him up, Madison appeared at the doorway. And she didn't look herself. She looked tired, pale and worried.

What on earth had happened in his absence? He hadn't been away long. Three and a bit days. That wasn't enough time for life to go pear-shaped.

Was it?

'Hello, Maddie.' He leaned forward and stole a kiss. 'Are you all right, *kardia mou*?'

'Just had a bit of a rough day.'

It sounded like rather more than that to him, but he didn't push it. 'Come on. We'll go somewhere quiet where the food's good.'

She bit her lip. 'Actually, Theo, I'm not sure I want anything to eat.'

He frowned. 'Are you coming down with a bug or something?'

'No-o.'

But she didn't sound too sure. 'Maddie, what's wrong?' he asked.

She took a deep breath. 'There isn't an easy way to say this. And my doorstep isn't the right place either. Look, can we go and sit in the park across the road?'

'Sure.' Unease prickled down his spine. She definitely

didn't sound herself—or look that pleased about seeing him again. Had she had time to think about it and decided that being with him would be a mistake?

He shook himself. Speculating on the situation wasn't going to help at all. So he did as she'd asked: he walked with her across to the park and sat next to her on a bench.

'Tell me what's wrong,' he said as gently as he could, forcing the panic back.

She bit her lip. 'Theo…I'm pregnant.'

He stared at her, unable to believe he'd heard her correctly. 'Run that by me again.'

'I'm pregnant. Expecting our baby.'

Pregnant.

No, no, no.

This couldn't be happening.

Please, let him be dreaming.

But when he pinched his own arm surreptitiously, it hurt—so he knew that he was definitely awake. This was real. 'You're pregnant?' he echoed, hoping he'd misheard or misunderstood yet knowing at the same time that his English was flawless and there was no way he could have misunderstood her.

She nodded, looking anxious.

This was the last thing he'd expected. And it knocked him sideways. He raked a hand through his hair. 'We were careful. So there must have been a problem with the condom.'

'Don't hate me, Theo.'

'Of course I don't hate you!' He *loved* her. Though now didn't feel like the right time to say so.

He didn't want her thinking it was a knee-jerk reaction to the news.

'I know how you feel about babies.' Her face looked pinched. 'I didn't do it on purpose, Theo.'

'I know.' He tried to smile reassuringly at her. But inside he was panicking. Madison was pregnant. With his baby.

His worst nightmare.

This wasn't how it was meant to happen.

He'd intended to come home, tell her he loved her and ask her to marry him.

Now… Well, he was just going to have to face this one on his own and be brave, for Madison's sake—to borrow a phrase from his sister, he had to take his courage in both hands. 'OK. We need to deal with this.'

She went white. 'Are you suggesting that I have a termination?'

'No, of course I'm not.' He stared at her in disbelief. 'What kind of man do you think I am? No. You're pregnant with my baby, so you're moving in with me.'

She blinked. 'Don't you boss me about, Theo Petrakis.'

'In my culture, a man looks after his woman.'

'I'm not your woman.'

'You're expecting my child. That makes you my woman.' As well as the love of his life. But right now he had a feeling she was too angry to hear that.

'Theo, you don't even want children!'

Actually, he did. Though the potential for catastrophe turned his stomach into knots. 'I don't have a choice in the matter.'

She lifted her chin. 'Yes, you do. You can walk away.'

'No, I can't. And I don't want to either. I'm not going to walk away from you, Maddie.' He reached across and took her hand. 'You're having my child. And no child of mine will have a single parent. You're going to marry me.'

'No way.' She shook her hand free.

What? But…he'd thought that was what she wanted. Marriage and babies. 'Why not?'

'We've only known each other a few weeks.'

Now he knew what the problem was.

And he knew the answer, too. He recaptured her hand. 'I know you got married to Harry in a rush, and it all went wrong, but this is different. I'm not Harry.'

'But it'll still go wrong. You said you don't want marriage and babies.' She lifted her chin. 'You'll resent me for trapping you.'

'You're not trapping me and I won't resent you, Maddie. Far from it. I want to look after you.'

She rolled her eyes. 'I'm a big girl. I can look after myself.'

'True. But you don't have to.' He sighed. 'Look, of course you have doubts. As I do. You're afraid. As I am. But it'll make a difference if we face this together. Because we'll be supporting each other, we'll get through the fear. We're a great team at work. And we're a great team outside work, too. The bits where I'm scared, you're brave. The bits where you're scared, I'm brave.'

She was silent, as if digesting his words.

He tried again. 'I'm not going to lie to you the way Harry did. I won't cheat on you, and I'm not going to make promises I won't keep. The bottom line is, you're having my baby and we're going to get married.'

She shook her head. 'There are plenty of single parents around. This is the twenty-first century. You don't have to get married any more just because you're having a baby.'

'It works like that in my country.'

'Well, we're in mine—which, as you have English grandparents, is half yours anyway,' she pointed out, 'so *tough*.'

'It *will* be tough, Maddie, going it alone. Especially because you don't have to. Look, you grew up with two parents.' He swallowed hard. 'So did I. Eventually. And I think that's healthy. In my view, a child is best off with two parents.'

'Not if the parents are going to argue all the time.'

'Have we argued before today?' he asked. 'I mean, seriously argued?'

'We're arguing now.'

He could see the glitter of tears in her eyes. Hell. He didn't want it to be this way. '*Matia mou*, I'm sorry. I'm making a mess of this. And I really didn't mean to hurt you.' He sighed. 'I don't think I can make this any worse right now, so I may as well…' He took the box from his pocket. 'Here. I bought you this in Greece.'

She frowned. 'I said you didn't need to bring me anything back.'

'This is different.' He put the box in her hands.

She was still frowning, but then she opened the box. Saw the ring sporting a pink stone cut in a heart shape. Looked at him with a hundred questions in her eyes. 'Theo?'

'It's an engagement ring, Maddie,' he said softly. 'Just so you know I'm not asking you to marry me because of the baby. I was going to ask you to marry me tonight anyway. Yes, I probably should have waited and chosen the ring with you, but I happened to see this and it was just so *you*. A pink diamond. Sparkly. Like the way you've put sparkle into my life.'

This time her eyes brimmed over and a tear trickled silently down her cheek. 'So you don't want to get married to me just because of the baby?'

'I didn't know about the baby when I bought the ring, *kardoula mou*. Yes, of course I want you for you.'

'Supposing it doesn't fit me?'

'Then we'll get it altered.' He looked levelly at her. 'Are you going to try it on?'

She swallowed hard. 'Theo, I need think about this.' She closed the box and handed it back to him.

'You don't like the ring?'

'I like the ring. I *love* the ring.' She dragged in a breath. 'But…my world's suddenly been turned upside down. I need some space, some time to think about this.'

He drew her hand up to his lips, kissed each finger in turn. 'All right. I'm not going to bully you into anything. But you know where I am if you want anything.'

'All I want to do right now is go home—to *my* home,' she emphasised, 'and get some sleep.'

'Have you eaten tonight?'

'You just said you weren't going to bully me.'

'I'm not bullying you,' he said quietly. 'I'm concerned. How pregnant are you?'

'It's really early days. I only realised and did the test, a couple of days ago. I'd say about…' She shrugged. 'Five weeks.'

He nodded. 'So morning sickness has probably just started—not that it's necessarily mornings only. Try some dry crackers or sipping flat ginger beer.'

'As an obstetrician,' she reminded him, 'I know that.'

'I know you do.' He smiled wryly. 'Force of habit. OK. I'm not going to nag. But you need to look after yourself.' He stroked her cheek. 'Or, better still, let me look after you.'

'Theo,' she warned, 'you're bullying.'

'I'm concerned about you, *matia mou*. You *and* the baby.' He stood up and drew her to her feet. 'Come on. I'll walk you home. Have an early night, sleep on it, and we can talk again tomorrow. Or if you wake up at stupid o'clock tonight and want to talk, you know my number.' He delivered her to her front door. Much as he wanted to pull her into his arms and kiss her stupid, kiss all her fears away, he knew it was a bad idea. If he rushed her now, when she had time to catch her breath she'd resent him for it. So instead he reined himself back. Kissed her chastely on the cheek. And suppressed the urge to pick her up and carry her back to his own house.

Theo wanted to marry her.

In her heart of hearts, Madison knew that was exactly what she wanted, too.

So why wasn't she excited and happy and wanting to shout the news from the rooftops? Why couldn't she make the fear go away—the fear that it would all go wrong?

After an hour of feeling more and more miserable, she texted Katrina. Diffidently, because she didn't want her to worry. But, lord, she needed to talk to someone about this. Someone close to her.

If you're not busy, do you want to come over for a cup of tea?

The answer came back almost immediately. *On my way.*

'Maddie? What's happened?' Katrina asked as Madison opened the door a little later. 'You look terrible.'

Maddie led her into the living room and slumped into one of the chairs 'Everything's going wrong. Theo just asked me to move in with him and get married.'

Katrina frowned. 'And that's wrong *how*, exactly?'

'I'm pregnant.'

'Hang on. Backtrack a bit. You're pregnant so he asked you to marry him?' Katrina's eyes widened. 'I'm going to be an auntie? How pregnant? When did you find out?'

'Sort of, yes, not very and the other day.' Madison answered the questions rapidly in order.

'Define "sort of".'

'He bought the ring before he knew about the baby,' Madison admitted.

'What ring?' Katrina looked pointedly at Madison's left hand.

'I gave it back to him.'

'Maddie, *why*? You love him.'

Madison sighed. 'Exactly. I'm not so sure he loves me.'

'You just told me he bought you the ring before you told him about the baby. So he must love you, or he wouldn't have wanted to marry you.'

'But he didn't say the words, Kat. And he's still got that brick wall up between us.'

'And you don't have a brick wall there, too?' Katrina asked.

'What do you mean?'

'You're looking for reasons to reject Theo—because you're scared that if you do get married to him it'll end up as much a mistake as your marriage to Harry.'

Madison sighed. 'Maybe.'

'There's no maybe about it, hon,' Katrina said. 'Look, I know he hasn't said the words, but he loves you. Give the landlord your notice and move in with Theo. What have you got to lose? And don't say your heart—because you've lost that to him already. Give it a try,' she urged. 'So when do I get to meet my niece or nephew?'

'I haven't booked in with the midwifery team yet, so I don't know the exact date,' Madison hedged.

Katrina scoffed. 'Says the obstetrician.'

'OK, OK. If I worked out my dates right, I'm due early February,' Madison said.

Katrina hugged her. 'Well, congratulations. And I want to be number one on your babysitting list.' Her smile faded. 'That is…as long as you get a really loud baby listener, one with lights.'

'That's a definite,' Madison said, knowing exactly what her cousin was worrying about and hugging her back. 'You're top of my godmother list, too.'

'I'm glad to hear it.' Katrina smiled at her. 'I'm really

pleased for you. You're going to be a brilliant mum. And I think Theo's going to be a great dad—and husband, if you let him.'

'And if it all goes wrong?'

'Then I'll be here for you,' Katrina said.

'Stop worrying. Get some sleep. And tomorrow you can talk to Theo and work out when you're going to move in with him.'

CHAPTER TWELVE

THEO was busy in clinic next morning, and he spent lunch-time and half the afternoon in one of the delivery rooms with a complicated labour. When he finally took a break, he discovered that Madison was in one of the other delivery rooms.

So it looked as if he'd have to be patient.

Something he was starting to find very, very difficult.

He grabbed a sandwich from the canteen and ate it at his desk while he caught up with paperwork. He'd just finished replying to a slew of emails when there was a rap on his open office door.

'Hi, there. I hear you missed lunch—so I thought you might need some supplies.' Madison walked in with a mug of strong black coffee and a blueberry muffin.

'Thanks.' He gestured to the door. 'Do you want to close that for a moment?'

She did so.

'How are you?' he asked.

'OK, as long as I stay away from the scent of this stuff.' She put the mug and plate on his desk, then sat down. 'I've been talking to Katrina. Thinking.'

'And?'

'And if the offer of moving in with you is still open, I'll give it a try.'

'The offer was marriage, Maddie.'

She shook her head. 'Don't rush me. I've been married before and it went wrong. This is a big thing for me, Theo.'

'It's a big thing for me, too, *matia mou*.' He smiled wryly. 'I haven't asked anyone to marry me before.'

'You didn't actually ask me,' she pointed out. 'You told me.'

'Ah. Then let me remedy that.' He went over to the blinds, closed them and locked his office door before returning to her side and dropping down on one knee. He fished the box from his pocket, opened it, then took her right hand and placed the box on it. 'Madison Gregory, would you do me the honour of becoming my wife?'

'I…' Her voice was croaky.

'I'm house-trained, I cook—a lot better than you do,' he said with a smile, 'and I promise you I'll never lie to you, Maddie.'

She swallowed hard. 'But supposing…?'

'Stop worrying,' he said softly. 'My family will adore you, I hope that yours will like me, and it really doesn't matter where or when wc get married. Right now, the most important things to me are you and our baby. Everything else is just a minor detail.'

'I don't want to wear a ring at work,' she said.

'Because you don't want people to know about us?' he asked carefully.

She shook her head. 'It's not that. I don't want the world to know about the baby until I'm twelve weeks and past the risky stage.'

Fair enough. He could understand that. Most of his mums-to-be said the same thing.

'And there's also the fact about what I do…I can't wear a ring when I'm examining a mum or helping with a delivery.'

Also true. He relaxed. So it wasn't that she didn't want to wear his ring. There was a chance this was going to work out.

'Sure. I'll buy you a platinum chain so you can wear it round your neck instead of on your finger when you're on duty, if you want to.'

'Platinum?' she queried.

'So it's the same metal as the ring—otherwise they're likely to damage each other.'

'This is *platinum*?' She looked at the ring again.

'Yes.'

'And the stone is…?'

'A diamond,' he told her. 'A pink one. And may I remind you that I'm still down on one knee here, and it's starting to get a little uncomfortable?'

'Um.'

He took the ring out of the box. 'Marry me, Maddie,' he said softly, and slid the ring onto the third finger of her left hand.

It was a perfect fit.

'Now that,' Theo said, 'is a good omen.'

'I guess so,' she admitted.

'Then are you going to put me out of my misery?'

'This whole thing scares me stupid, Theo,' she said.

'That makes two of us. So let's be scared together. I'm not Harry, Maddie. I'm not perfect either—I'm just a man. But I intend to be the best husband and father I can possibly be.'

Her eyes filled with tears. 'Oh, Theo.'

He stood up and pulled her into his arms, holding her close and hoping she'd be able to take strength from his closeness. 'So is that a yes?'

She dragged in a breath. 'Yes,' she whispered.

'Good.' He kissed her very gently. 'After work, we're going out to celebrate our engagement. You, me and a bottle of sparkling water.'

'No champagne?'

He smiled, pleased that she was recovering her equilibrium

enough to tease him. 'If you want half a glass of champagne, *agapi mou*, you can have it with pleasure. But if you don't like even the smell of coffee, my guess is you're not going to like champagne right now either.'

She smiled back. 'Fizzy water it is, then.'

The next week zoomed past. At the weekend Madison moved her belongings to Theo's house—or, rather, she directed and he moved them, because he refused to let her lift a single thing. He also insisted on driving her down to Suffolk on the Sunday afternoon to meet her family, and to her relief they adored him.

And living with Theo was even better than she could have dreamed. She loved falling asleep in his arms at night, feeling protected and safe. Admittedly, he still hadn't actually said he loved her, but he showed her in so many other ways. Like cooking bland foods for her so she could eat without feeling queasy, rubbing her back in exactly the right place even before she'd admitted that it ached, and making sure she didn't overdo things. And what were words after all? Harry had said he loved her, but he hadn't. Theo was definitely a man whose actions spoke louder than his words. She trusted him. So she really had to stop being silly and wishing he'd say he loved her. Stop being so needy.

Madison went to her booking-in appointment with the midwife on her own, but when her first blood tests came back, Theo looked at the results and frowned. 'You're rhesus negative.'

'Uh-huh.'

'I'm not.'

She looked at him. 'How do you know?'

'I'm a blood donor.'

She shrugged. 'Well, it doesn't matter. The baby hasn't necessarily inherited your blood group, and I haven't had a previous miscarriage or termination, so even if the baby's blood group is rhesus positive there's no reason why I'd be sensitised to rhesus positive blood. No antibodies showed up on the screening, did they?' She smiled. 'There is such a thing as anti-D immunoglobulin—which I'll have after the birth, and it'll mop up any rhesus positive blood cells that might have crossed into me, so there shouldn't be a problem in the future.'

'And you'll have more blood tests at twenty-eight and thirty-six weeks to make sure all's well—and you'll probably have anti-D in the last three weeks just to cover any of the little "silent" bleeds that happen in late pregnancy.' He grimaced. 'I know. I'm getting worried over nothing.'

She took his hand. 'Theo, was your mum rhesus negative?'

'No. So don't start worrying on that score.' He smiled wryly. 'I'm worrying enough for both of us there, OK?'

No, it wasn't OK. Because every time she tried to bring up the subject of his mother and reassure him that she was going to be perfectly fine, he distracted her. Threw up a brick wall. She knew he was trying to protect her from his fears, but it drove her crazy.

She still hadn't managed to persuade Theo to talk about it by the beginning of August when she went for the dating scan, though this time he came to the antenatal appointment with her. And she noticed that Theo blinked back tears when he saw the image of their baby moving on the radiographer's screen.

'Considering how many times you've seen one of these over the years, Mr Petrakis,' she teased, 'you should be used to them by now.'

He held her hand tightly. 'I know. But it's the first time I've seen *my* baby.' He stared at the screen. 'It's incredible.'

'Most dads are the same. They can't quite believe it,' the radiographer said with a smile. 'I take it you'd both like pictures?'

'Lots and lots and lots,' Theo said. 'Because I know some

grandparents, aunties and uncles who are going to insist on having their own copies.'

He called his parents that evening to tell them the news and emailed them the scan pictures while he was on the phone. In response, they flew over at the weekend to meet Maddie. And any fears she might've had that they wouldn't like her vanished within the first ten seconds of meeting them: Georgios had brought her the most enormous bouquet of roses she'd ever seen, and Eleni gave her a huge, tight hug. 'I'm so pleased my boy has finally found someone. Even if he has kept you incredibly quiet.'

'Well, I had to do something to stop you throwing heiresses at me,' Theo declared.

She cuffed his arm. 'We did nothing of the kind. We just wanted you to settle down and have a family and be as happy as we are.' She beamed. 'And now we've met you, Maddie, I know for sure he will.'

It didn't get any better than this, Madison thought. Especially when Theo started to relax and plan a nursery with her. He was the one who booked their antenatal classes and found out all the information about gentle antenatal water exercise classes for her. He even surprised her by coming home late one evening and admitting that he'd spent an hour with Iris, their senior midwife, and she'd taught him how to massage a pregnant woman and which oils were safe to use.

Life was perfect.

Until the end of September, when Madison was on a day off and her midwife rang. 'Maddie? I just wondered if I could pop round and see you, love.'

She froze. Community midwives were incredibly busy. They didn't just offer to pop round and see you for a cup of tea—not unless there was something they needed to discuss. 'What's wrong?'

'Just something I want to discuss with you.'

Just as she'd feared. And she knew exactly what it was likely to be, too. 'Oh, hell. It's the triple test results, isn't it?' The test that showed the possibility of the baby having a condition such as spina bifida or Down's syndrome.

The midwife sighed. 'That's the thing about having a maternity specialist as a client—you know as much as I do. Yes, love, I'm afraid it is. Your results are borderline.'

'How borderline?'

'One in ninety.'

That wasn't borderline. Especially for her age. A one in ninety chance of a medical condition…

Madison knew that the only way she was going to get through this was to pretend it was happening to someone else. To one of her mums-to-be instead of to herself. So she switched into professional mode. 'I'll talk to my partner and call you back to let you know if we want an amniocentesis.' A further test, which would tell them for certain whether their baby had either condition. But it was an invasive test, one with a risk of miscarriage. Given that Theo had been worried about her pregnancy to start with, this was going to make him worry even more.

'I'd feel a lot better about this if I came round for a chat,' the midwife said.

'No need. I know what the options are.' Madison made her voice sound as bright as possible. 'I'm absolutely fine. Really.'

It took all her skill to persuade her midwife that everything was fine. When she finally put the phone down, what she really wanted to do was go straight to the hospital and see Theo. But that wouldn't be fair. He had a list of people waiting to see him. She'd just take it easy and wait for him to come home.

She managed to last out until mid-afternoon. And then she called his office.

'Theo Petrakis,' he said absently, as if he'd answered the

phone in the middle of writing a report. Which, knowing Theo, he probably had.

'It's Maddie.'

'Is everything all right, *matia mou*?'

'We got the triple test results back this morning.'

'And?'

'One in ninety.'

Madison thought she'd sounded calm and collected, but clearly she hadn't, because Theo said immediately, 'I'm on my way.'

He was home much quicker than she'd expected; the door banged closed, and then he was there, holding her.

'I'm here, *agapi mou*,' he said softly. 'It's going to be OK. Everything's fine.'

'One in ninety. Theo, that's scary.'

'I've seen much scarier odds than that—and so have you, I'm sure—and everything was fine. I had a mum with a one in thirty result once, and she had the most beautiful little boy—a little boy with no medical conditions whatsoever. So try not to worry.'

She swallowed hard. 'I know.'

He stroked her hair. 'But it's easier when you're reassuring someone else. When it isn't *your* baby.' He drew her over to the sofa. 'When did the midwife ring?'

'This morning.'

'Why didn't you call me then, *matia mou*?'

She sighed. 'You were busy at work. In clinic.'

'I'm never too busy for you. Ever,' he told her, his eyes glittering.

She dragged in a breath. 'Sorry. I was trying to do the right thing. Be professional.'

'Sometimes you need to put yourself first,' he said gently. 'So what do you want to do?'

'It's been going round and round in my head all day. I…' She shook her head. 'I don't know.'

'Right now, we don't know what's happening. You could have an amniocentesis so we know for sure—so we can either relax and stop worrying—or we can prepare ourselves for our child's possible special needs.'

But the idea of it clearly worried him sick. Although he tried to mask it, she could see it in his face. 'You're thinking about the risks, aren't you?'

He sighed. 'It's an invasive procedure.'

One where a needle would go through her abdomen to take a sample of amniotic fluid containing the baby's cells, which would then be grown and studied in a lab. The procedure meant there was risk of tiny amounts of the baby's blood mixing with her own bloodstream. And if the baby's blood group was rhesus positive, there was a chance her body would start making antibodies—which would cross the placenta and attack the baby's red cells. And Madison knew they were both well aware of what that could lead to. Anaemia…and even foetal death.

'They can give me anti-D as a preventative measure.'

'True.' He paused. 'The chances are, everything will be fine.'

'But we won't know for sure. And I don't want to spend the next eighteen weeks worrying.' She swallowed hard. 'The only way we'll know for sure is if we have the amnio.'

'Is that what you want?'

She nodded. 'I've been thinking about it all day. I know there's a risk because of the blood thing and there's a risk of miscarriage with an amnio, but I think this is the right thing to do.'

'Then that's what we'll do. Do you want me to call the midwife?'

'No, I'll do it.'

'I can do the procedure, if you want me to,' he offered. 'I've got a lower than average record of miscarriages.'

'No. You're a brilliant doctor, Theo Petrakis. But you're also the father of my baby so it would be unethical.' She dragged in a breath. 'And anyway I want you right beside me, holding my hand while that needle goes in. Do you know how big that needle is?'

'I do, honey.' He kissed her lightly. 'It'll be a scratch, that's all. And, of course, I'll be there with you, holding your hand all the way through it.'

'Think of it as a practice for labour. When I'm going to crush your hand and scream at you during every contraction.'

He laughed. 'That's my job as a dad-to-be.' He sobered slightly. 'Whatever happens, Maddie, remember I'm always going to be there. Right by your side. So go and call the midwife, *matia mou*. I'll make you some hot blackcurrant.'

By the time he'd returned from the kitchen, everything was arranged. 'Tomorrow afternoon, half-past two.'

'Fine. I'll book some time off.' He paused. 'And maybe I can distract you a bit with some news.'

'What news?'

'Doug isn't coming back. He's fine—it's not a relapse or anything,' Theo hastened to reassure her, 'but he's decided he wants to move out of London with his family and take a bit of time to smell the roses.'

'So what happens now?'

Theo shrugged. 'Applications for the job are invited.'

She went very still. 'Are you going to apply?'

'That,' he said, 'is entirely up to you. I can apply for the job—or I can apply to a different hospital in London. Or we can move down to Suffolk to be nearer your family and I'll find a job there.'

'You'd move? For me?'

'If that's what you want, *agapi mou*.' He smiled at her. 'Now stop worrying. Everything's going to be fine.'

* * *

Just as he'd promised, he took time off to be with Madison for the amniocentesis. He held her hand while she lay on the couch, talking softly to her. 'Just try to relax. You'll feel a sharp scratch but it's not going to hurt, and it's not going to hurt the baby. The ultrasonographer's going to take just a tiny, tiny little bit of amniotic fluid, and the baby won't even miss it.'

Madison swallowed hard. 'I know the theory.'

'But the practice feels incredibly scary when it's you,' he said wryly. 'I know, *matia mou*. But it's going to be fine.'

'Try to relax, Dr Gregory,' the ultrasonographer said. 'Then the baby will settle down, too. Look up at the mobile.'

Madison smiled. 'Dolphins.'

Theo glanced at the screen. 'You're still jumpy, *kardoula mou*. You need to relax so the baby relaxes, too. OK. Let's bring in the big guns.' To Madison's surprise, he started singing. In Greek. She had no idea what the words meant, but the tune was soft and sweet and calming, and Theo had a gorgeous voice.

She hadn't had the faintest idea that he could sing.

And it worked, because the ultrasonographer inserted the needle into her bump. 'OK. All done. We'll call you as soon as we get the results—well, you know the drill.'

'We do,' Theo said. 'And I'm going to take Maddie home for two days of bed rest.'

'Good idea,' the ultrasonographer said. 'Try not to worry, Dr Gregory. In most cases everything is absolutely fine. And do you want to know whether it's a boy or a girl?'

Madison glanced at Theo.

'Your choice, *agapi mou*,' he said softly.

'Then, yes, please. We'd like to know,' Madison said.

The ultrasonographer wrote a note in the file. 'I see you're rhesus negative,' she said. 'So you know what this means.'

'Anti-D,' Madison said wryly. 'Though I'm glad it's a much smaller needle than the one you just used.'

When she'd been given the injection, Theo said, 'Sit here for five minutes and catch your breath. I'll call the taxi.'

He was steamrollering her again. And he was honestly expecting she'd submit to two days' bed rest?

She was simmering all the way home.

And she exploded when Theo insisted that she go straight to bed.

'You're making a ridiculous fuss! Of course I don't need to be in bed.'

'Yes, you do. It's called taking it easy.'

'I can do that sitting on the sofa, if I have to.'

He folded his arms. 'There's no "if" about it, Maddie. You know as well as I do that after an invasive procedure you need to take it easy. Do I have to spell it out for you?'

She knew what he meant. The risk of miscarrying their baby. 'No.'

'You're going on bed rest for two days, and that's that.'

'That's outrageous.'

His mouth set in a thin line. 'Has it occurred to you, Maddie, that I might be worried sick about you and about the baby, and I'm trying as hard as I can to be calm about it so I can support you through your worries instead of focusing on my own? So do me a favour and be sensible about this.'

She had a feeling that there was more to it than that. 'This is about your mum, isn't it?'

'Hardly.'

He was being evasive, she was sure. 'Then why don't you tell me? Talk to me, Theo. Don't shut me out. Not now.'

He was silent for a long, long time. And then he sighed. 'Come and lie down. And then I'll tell you everything.'

She allowed him to shepherd her upstairs and sat on the bed. 'Talk to me,' she said.

'Given that you've just had an amniocentesis, this isn't exactly a tactful subject,' he warned. 'You know my mum died very shortly after she had me.' He dragged in a breath. 'She had an amniotic fluid embolism.'

She blinked. 'Theo, that really wasn't your fault. And AFEs are incredibly rare.'

'My head knows that. But my heart...I know how my father felt every time Eleni was pregnant—because I went straight into panic mode when you told me you were expecting our baby.'

'And the rhesus negative business is a complication, so it makes things worse.'

'Yes,' he admitted.

She stroked his face. 'First of all, I'm having anti-D so there's nothing to worry about as far as the baby's concerned. Secondly, it's so unlikely that I'll have an AFE—you've got more chance of going to the moon, Theo. Medicine's advanced an awful lot since you were a baby.'

'I know. I want our baby, Maddie, I really do—but I'm terrified I'm going to lose you because of the baby, the way my dad lost my mum. I'm an obstetrician. I know all the possible complications.'

'You also know how rare they are.' She reached up to kiss him. 'We see the complicated cases. How many straightforward births are there where the midwives don't need us at all?'

'I know. But I still can't get it through to here.' He took her hand and laid it across his heart. 'What I'm saying is that if I lose you my life isn't going to mean anything any more. Just ashes. Because I love you so much.'

Finally he'd said it.

In circumstances she would never have imagined in her wildest dreams.

'And that's why you're driving me insane?' she asked. 'Because you love me?'

'Because I love you,' he confirmed. 'And that's the reason why I'm being over-protective.'

'Oh, Theo.' She cuddled into him.

'So, whether you like it or not, you're staying put for the next two days.' He smiled. 'I'm going to be here to make sure of it.'

'How? You're supposed to be at work.'

'I've organised a locum. Because you're more important to me than anything else. Even the baby.'

She dragged in a breath. 'Nothing's going to happen to me—but if the unthinkable does happen, what then, Theo? I need to know that you won't react the way your dad did. That you'll love our baby and cherish him—or her—for my sake, not just hand the baby to my parents or yours and walk away.'

'Hey, now you're at it. Being morbid. And I'm supposed to keep you happy and rested.' He kissed her forehead. 'Sorry, I've made such a mess of this.'

'You haven't reassured me yet.'

'I promise,' he said softly. 'I'll love our baby and cherish him or her. Because it'll be our baby.'

'But nothing's going to happen to me. Got that?'

'Got that.'

'You love me.' She shook her head in wonderment.

'I fell in love with you the first moment I met you,' he said softly. 'There was something about you. Just…I'm not so good with words.'

She scoffed. 'Your English is perfect. You're half-English, for pity's sake.'

He nodded. 'That's one of the reasons why Dad insisted I learn English. The French, German, Spanish and Italian were just in case I took over from him.'

She blinked. 'You speak *six* languages? Oh, don't you ever tell me you're not good with words again!'

He coughed. 'Someone not too far from here isn't too good with words either.'

'What do you mean?'

'S'agapo. Je t'aime. Ich liebe dich. Te quiero. Ti amo.' He spread his hands. 'And now I've told you in six languages, is there something you might want to say to me?'

She laughed. 'You're such a show-off.'

'That wasn't *quite* what I was angling for,' he said ruefully.

She kissed him lightly on the lips. 'Do you really not know how I feel about you? I love you, Theo. Part of me's scared stupid because I fell for you so quickly, and when I let Harry sweep me off my feet I made the worst mistake in my life. But I know that keeping you at arm's length would be an even bigger mistake—because you're not like Harry. You put me first.'

'And our baby,' he said softly. 'You're my world, Maddie. I can't promise that I'm not going to worry until the baby's born, and I can't promise that I won't go straight into panic mode next time you tell me you're pregnant.'

'Next time?' she queried.

'Next time,' he said. 'Katrina's as close as a sister to you but I'd guess that, being an only child, you want more than one baby.'

'And you'd be prepared to put yourself through all the worry for me?' she asked.

'Yes. Because you'll be beside me, all the way,' he said simply.

CHAPTER THIRTEEN

TO THEO'S relief, Madison submitted to spending two days on bed rest. And telling her the last bit of his fears—the deepest, darkest ones he'd tried to keep buried, for her sake—seemed to have made them go away.

He was sorting out paperwork at his desk when his pager went off. He glanced at the reading. Emergency department.

He rang straight down. 'Theo Petrakis from Maternity. You paged me.'

'It's Ed, Theo. I've got an ambulance on its way, ETA about seven minutes, with a mum-to-be who was a passenger in a car accident. She's thirty-four weeks and can feel the baby move, but she's got stomach pains, her heart rate's up a bit, and the ambulance crew reports that she's pale.'

Could be premature labour, could be stress—but Theo had a nasty feeling about this one. Given her symptoms and the circumstances, it was possibly a placental abruption, where the accident caused the placenta to come away from the wall of the womb. The loss of blood would cause her pallor.

'OK. Tell the crew not to do a vaginal exam until we've had a chance to do an ultrasound and we're sure that it's not placenta praevia. Are there any obvious signs of blood?'

'Hold on, I'll get patched through.' There was a pause. 'No.'

Which meant it could be a 'hidden' abruption, with a huge blood clot behind the placenta. The most complicated sort—and the one with one of the highest risks. 'OK. I'm on my way down. We need a scanner, and I'll get Iris to sort out Theatre just in case. Ask the crew to secure IV access and if she's going into shock get her on oxygen. As soon as she comes in, I want six units of blood cross-matched.'

'Will do. Thanks, Theo.'

Theo hung up and left his office. To his relief, Iris was at the reception desk with Madison. 'Iris, I'm on my way down to the emergency department. I might need to do an emergency section, so can you get me a theatre and anaesthetist on standby?'

'I'm on it,' Iris said, picking up the phone.

'Do you want me with you?' Madison asked. 'If you're doing an emergency section, you'll need someone to assist.'

He grimaced. 'Maddie, I'm not sure this is a case for you.'

'It's my job,' she reminded him. 'And I'm pregnant, not incompetent. I can put my feelings aside for work. If anything, I might be able to help more because my bump might help reassure the mum that I know exactly how she feels.'

And it would also mean she was kept too busy to think about the test results: exactly the same technique he was using. 'OK. But I reserve the right to ask someone to take over from you if I think it's going to upset you too much.'

'All right. So what's happened?' she asked as they made their way down to the emergency department.

'Mum-to-be was a passenger and their car was involved in a crash. No sign of a bleed, but she's got cramps, tachycardia and pallor.'

'You're thinking an abruption?'

'Could be.' Theo sighed. 'If it's concealed or severe, we could be looking at DIC—in which case there's no time to give steroids to help mature the baby's lungs.'

The expression on his face meant that Madison made a final connection. This must have been what had happened to Theo's mum after the embolism. She would have gone into DIC—disseminated intravascular coagulation, meaning that the clotting factors in the blood were activated throughout the body instead of being localised to the site of the injury. So small blood clots developed throughout the body, using up the blood's clotting factors so it couldn't clot where it was really needed.

Every time he had to deal with a case like this, it must rip his heart to pieces. Doubly so, now that he was a dad-to-be.

'It's going to be all right,' she said softly, taking his hand briefly and squeezing it.

'I'm going to try my damnedest to make sure it does.'

There was the tiniest, tiniest crack in his voice. Nobody else would have noticed it, she was sure. But she had.

But by the time they'd reached the emergency department there was no fear or emotion in his face. Theo was cool and calm and so very reassuring when he introduced them both to the patient.

'Mrs Staveley, I'm Theo Petrakis, the senior consultant obstetrician, and this is my colleague, Maddie Gregory.'

Mrs Staveley pulled the oxygen mask from her face. 'My baby. Please tell me my baby's going to be all right,' she begged, her face absolutely white.

'I know you're worried,' Theo said gently, 'and that's why we're here. If you don't mind, I'd like to examine you while Maddie does a few checks on you, and I'd also like to give you an ultrasound so we can see exactly what's going on. And keep that mask on for me, because it's going to help you breathe and make you feel a lot better.'

Madison took Mrs Staveley's blood pressure and checked her heart rate while Theo examined her abdomen. Although his expression didn't change, she caught the concern in his eyes, and she guessed that Mrs Staveley's abdomen was tense and 'woody' to the touch. Given that her blood pressure was low and she was still tachycardic, this was looking more and more like a case of abruption.

Quietly, she gave Theo the figures. He nodded, but kept the concern out of his face. 'Thanks, Maddie. Mrs Staveley, I'm going to rub a little bit of gel on your tummy now—it'll feel a little bit cold. And then we'll take a look at the baby. Can you still feel the baby moving?'

Mrs Staveley nodded.

'That's a good sign,' Madison said, holding her hand. 'I know you're worried—it's only natural after what you've been through—but you're in good hands. Theo's the best.'

Theo put the head of the transponder unit over Mrs Staveley's abdomen. 'One baby. And I can see the baby moving, so try not to worry.'

Maddie, who could also see the screen, mentally counted the baby's heartbeats and winced inwardly. This wasn't good. Particularly as nothing else on the scan seemed wrong. Theo's hunch about a concealed abruption was proving to be right.

Theo removed the transponder and wiped her skin clean. 'I want to keep an eye on your baby's heart rate, so I'm going to put a monitor on your tummy. Is that OK?'

She nodded.

He took her hand gently. 'I think that in the accident your placenta came away from the wall of your womb. We can't see it on the scan, but your blood pressure's dropping and your heart's beating too quickly, so that tells me you have what we call a concealed placental abruption—the blood's collecting behind the placenta instead of giving nutrients and oxygen to the baby. So what I need to do is give you a blood transfusion and put a catheter in so we can check your urine, then take you up to Theatre and deliver your baby.'

Mrs Staveley grabbed the mask and dragged it away from her mouth and nose. 'You can't, it's too soon!'

'You're thirty-four weeks, yes?'

She nodded.

'Your baby might need a little time in special care to help with breathing, but that's normal for babies born this early. We deliver babies much earlier than this and they're absolutely fine, so try not to worry.'

'Is there someone we can call for you?' Madison asked.

'My husband… Except he's at work.'

'Give me his number and we'll call him,' Madison said.

'But I'm afraid we can't wait for him to get here before we deliver the baby,' Theo warned gently. 'I might need to give you a Caesarean, in which case you'll need a general anaesthetic and your husband won't be able to come into Theatre, but we'll keep him informed and bring him to see you as soon as possible.'

Madison wrote down Mr Staveley's number while Theo said quietly to Ed, 'We need a haematologist, fresh frozen plasma if we can get it or fibrinogen if we can't. Also a neonatal specialist, plus put the special care baby unit on standby. And we need to stabilise her before we take her to Theatre—are the cross-matched units here yet?'

'I'm on it,' Ed said.

'Maddie, I want you to keep an eye on Mrs Staveley's blood pressure, urine output and the foetal heartbeat, OK?'

'Will do.'

Theo talked Mrs Staveley through the procedures, then inserted a catheter before giving her a transfusion.

'Systolic pressure, Maddie?'

'Seventy-eight.'

'Right. We're looking at at least fifteen hundred mils. Ed, the blood?'

'Here,' the registrar said.

'Great. Keep this going through. Maddie, what can you tell me?'

She gave him the figures, knowing they would mean little to Mrs Staveley but Theo would know the baby was in distress. 'Systolic's 100.'

'Great. We're there.' He took Mrs Staveley's hand. 'We're taking you up to Theatre now, and the anaesthetist's meeting us there,' he said gently. 'You're doing really well. But I'm going to have to deliver the baby by Caesarean section. It means you're going to be asleep through the operation, but this is the safest thing for you and for the baby.'

Although a vaginal delivery would be better for the mother, the baby was in distress and they didn't have time to wait—if they left it much longer, Mrs Staveley was likely to develop a clotting disorder, and that could be disastrous. Even though Madison knew just what an emergency this Caesarean section was, Theo maintained an aura of calm and stopped their mum-to-be worrying.

And then the anaesthetist was talking to Mrs Staveley and the theatre nurse was preparing her for the operation while Theo and Madison scrubbed up. 'We're going to have to be quick about this,' Theo said. 'The baby's in distress, and we need to keep an eye on Mrs Staveley as well. I need hot packs, and we're going to have to hope that the bleeding stops with a quick delivery, or we might end up having to give her a hysterectomy.'

They'd worked together in Theatre before, and Maddie knew just how good Theo was. Given his excellent working relationship with the haematology department and Neonatal, she was sure this was going to work out with the right result.

Unless the abruption was much, much worse than they suspected. She knew Theo would make sure the monitoring was good enough that DIC wouldn't take them by surprise, but things could happen so fast in an operating theatre…

She damped the fears down. They weren't going to lose the mum or the baby. She believed in Theo absolutely.

After an urgent haematological consultation, Theo gave fibrinogen and fresh frozen plasma to help the blood clot at the moment of delivery, performed the operation and handed the baby over to Erin, the neonatal specialist, who was ready and waiting. 'It's a girl,' he said.

'Do you think…?' Madison asked in a whisper.

'We were in time? I hope so. But I'll be happier when I hear that first cry,' Theo said.

As if on cue, there was a thin little wail, and Madison smiled. 'There you go. Just waiting for your order.'

'Hmm. We're not out of the woods yet,' Theo warned softly. He turned to the haematologist. 'Bill, how's it looking?'

'Urine output's OK, just. Blood's clotting in seven minutes so we're on the border of OK. How's the uterus looking?'

'Atonic. We're going to have to help her contract.'

'Oxytocin,' the anaesthetist said. 'I'll give it now. Has the bleeding stopped?'

'Yes.'

'Good. No heparin,' Bill said. 'An ampoule of prostaglandin would be good now. Intravenously.'

'On it,' Theo said. 'And I'll compress the uterus manually. Maddie, can you help with this?'

'On it,' Madison said.

'Blood pressure?' Theo asked.

'Stable. You can close. We'll tell you if anything changes,' the anaesthetist said.

Theo started the long task of stitching up the incision. 'How's the baby doing?' he asked Erin as he worked.

'The Apgar score's as good as expected. She's holding her

own. We'll transfer her to SCBU.' She smiled. 'As soon as the mum's up to it, she can come in and see her baby. But can you prepare her for lots of noise, monitoring and tubes, and tell her it isn't anywhere near as scary as it looks?'

'Will do,' Madison said.

There was a tense moment when Mrs Staveley's blood pressure started to drop, but after another transfusion Bill and the anaesthetist pronounced her stable.

'Are you all right?' Theo asked Madison as they cleaned up afterwards.

'Sure. You did a fantastic job, Theo.'

'The team did a fantastic job,' he corrected. 'Including you. But you're looking shattered. You've had enough. Go home—and that's a work order, so you have to do what I say,' he added.

'How about a compromise? I'll go when Mrs Staveley comes round.'

'As long as you sit down right now.'

'Bossy,' she grumbled, but she knew he was right. The small of her back was beginning to ache slightly.

When Mrs Staveley had come round from the anaesthetic, Theo sat next to her and held her hand. 'Mrs Staveley, I'm delighted to tell you that you have a beautiful little girl. She's a good weight for her age, and Erin—she's the consultant in the special care baby unit—says she's holding her own.'

'Can I see her?'

'Not just yet,' Theo said. 'Not because there's a problem with her, but because we've had a few worries about you—you needed a couple of transfusions, and you need to rest under close observation for a while.'

'I want to see my baby.' A tear trickled down her cheek. 'I...I'm sorry, I'm being pathetic.'

'Don't apologise. You've been through the mill,' Theo said. 'If it'll help, I'll go and see your baby myself and take a

Polaroid, so you can see for yourself. But I do have some good news. Your husband's outside.' He smiled gently. 'And he's pretty desperate to see you. I'll go and fetch him, and then I'll go and check on the baby for you and report back.'

'My baby's really going to be all right?' Mrs Staveley asked Madison.

'She's in the best hands right now. And Erin says you can see your little girl any time you like—so as soon as Theo's happy to let you be moved, we can get a wheelchair and take you to see her.' She paused. 'They'll be giving her oxygen to help her breathe, and because they keep a close eye on all the babies in the unit you'll see a lot of wires and tubes and monitors—it looks a lot scarier than it really is,' Madison reassured her.

Mrs Staveley looked at her, and Madison saw the exact moment that her patient realised that she, too, was pregnant. 'You're expecting.'

'Nineteen weeks,' Madison confirmed.

Mrs Staveley swallowed. 'Doesn't it scare you, doing what you do?'

'Because I know all the worst-case scenarios, you mean?' Madison smiled. 'A little. But, then, there are a lot more mums who have uncomplicated labours. And I know all the midwives and all the doctors in the maternity unit, so I know I'm going to be in good hands.'

'Especially Dr Petrakis.'

Madison smiled. 'He's the best doctor I know.'

Theo brought Mr Staveley in to see his wife, and he and Madison withdrew to a discreet distance.

'You did a deal with me,' Theo reminded Madison. 'Mrs Staveley's conscious again, she's reunited with her husband and I'm going to see her baby and bring her a Polaroid back. So you're going home.'

'Theo—'

'Don't argue.' He stroked her face. 'You look tired, honey. And that's not fair on you or the baby.' He sighed. 'Sorry. I shouldn't have let you be on this case.'

'In high-risk cases, you need a registrar to assist you. Which would be me. It's my job, Theo.'

'But this was upsetting.'

'For you, too—I saw the look in your eyes before you switched to obstetrician mode.' She paused. 'You can't shield me from the difficult cases, Theo. It's my job.'

'True. But I want you to go home now and rest—and I *mean* rest, or I'll tell Katrina and she'll tell your mum who'll nag you stupid.' He kissed her lightly. 'I'll be home when I can. I need to be here for now.'

She knew why—if there were any post-operative complications, they were more likely to show up in the next couple of hours. 'OK. I'll see you when I see you.'

Madison was sitting with her feet up on the sofa when Theo called. 'Everything's fine, though I've told the ward to call me if there's any change,' he told her. 'And, Maddie—the Staveleys want to call their daughter Thea.'

'After you?' She felt the tears pricking her eyes. 'That's lovely.'

'I'm coming home now. Have you eaten?'

'I was starving, so yes. But I can cook something for you.'

He laughed. 'Honey, now I know you love me, if you're offering to go into the kitchen and cook something willingly. Don't worry. I'll call the pizza place and get something delivered for about ten minutes after I'm due in.'

'And garlic dough balls,' Madison said.

He laughed again. 'At least you're having a reasonable pregnancy craving. See you soon, *matia mou*.'

And as soon as he was home, he wrapped her in his arms. 'I'm so glad to be home with you, Maddie. Today was one of the worst emergencies we could've had.'

'And you got her back, Theo.'

'The team got her back,' he corrected. 'And it's made me realise. I'm still panicking inside that something might go wrong…but if it does, the chances are very, very good that you and the baby will both be absolutely fine.'

'I'm glad you realise that.' She paused. 'But we still have to get the results of the amnio.'

'Whatever they are, we'll get through it,' he said, stroking her face. 'I love you, Maddie, and I love our baby, and nothing's going to change that.'

CHAPTER FOURTEEN

EVERYTHING was fine...until the day the amniocentesis results were due.

When they heard nothing, Theo spent the evening pacing about, unable to settle. 'I can't stand this waiting. Tomorrow I'm going to look it up on the system at work,' he declared, scowling.

'Theo, you know as well as I do it takes at least three weeks to grow the cells. Today's the earliest we could hear—it might take another few days.'

Which would drive him absolutely crazy.

'We just have to wait. Besides, using the system like that at work is unethical. Not to mention it'll get you into trouble with data protection and what have you,' Madison pointed out.

He raised an eyebrow. 'Don't tell me you weren't thinking exactly the same thing.'

'Actually, no.' Her face looked slightly pinched. 'I'm too scared to see what's there. This isn't like exam results, where I always knew roughly how I'd done. This is nature—and I have no control whatsoever over it.'

He understood exactly how she felt. Madison had managed to reassure him—now it was his turn to reassure her. 'Whatever the results show, Maddie, it won't change how I feel about you.' He came to join her on the sofa, taking both her hands in his. 'If we're lucky and the results are fine, we're going to celebrate.'

'And if they're not fine?' Her voice was a cracked whisper.

'Then we have a lot of talking to do. Decisions to make.' Very difficult decisions. 'But believe me when I tell you that I love you—and, whatever happens, we're going to get through this. Together.'

Theo slept badly that night, lying awake next to Madison and wishing that he had some kind of magic wand to make everything all right. It took every ounce of effort to concentrate on his clinic the next morning; and when he'd finished, he went to find Madison.

'Any news?' he asked.

She shook her head.

'Right. Come with me.' He shepherded her into his office.

'Theo, you can't!'

'I'm not touching my computer.' He tapped the number of the laboratory into his phone. 'I'm talking to the boffins.'

She cut the connection. 'Theo, they won't tell you. You're not my consultant.'

'No.' He felt his shoulders sag. 'Maddie, this is driving me crazy.'

'I'll talk to them,' she said softly. 'We shouldn't really be doing this. We're going behind Joe's back.'

'Joe is in a delivery room.' He'd already checked on the consultant's whereabouts. 'We can't exactly haul him out to ask if he's got the results back. So this is the more professional way of doing it.'

She sighed. 'Give me the phone. I'll do it.'

He sat down, scooped her onto his lap and let her take the phone. She hit the redial button, connected to the lab and asked about her results.

And Theo wished he'd been thinking straight enough to ask

her to put the phone on speaker mode rather than use the handset. He was going crazy, waiting to find out what was going on.

'OK,' Madison said. Her breath hitched. 'Thank you.'

And then she put the phone down and burst into tears.

Oh, hell. Clearly it was bad news. He wrapped his arms round her, holding her tightly. '*Agapi mou*, it will be all right. I'm here. I love you. And we'll get through this. We'll talk it through and we'll make the right decision for us.'

She was still shaking. 'Not bad news,' she mumbled against his chest. 'Not bad.'

'What?' He didn't understand.

'It's fine.'

'When you're crying your eyes out, *kardoula mou*?'

'I'm crying with relief,' she explained, her voice shaky. 'The tests are fine. And we're… Oh, Theo. We're going to have a little girl.'

He held her even more tightly. 'A little girl. Just like her beautiful mother.'

'With her daddy's gorgeous smile.'

Tears were still running down Madison's face. He wiped them away with the pad of his thumb, and kissed her gently. 'We're going out to lunch to celebrate.' He glanced at his watch. 'And I think the quickest way to tell everyone is to text them.'

'I'll page Kat—she won't have her mobile phone switched on,' Madison said. 'I can't believe we've been so lucky.'

'And we're going to get luckier still,' he promised.

The following day, it seemed his words had been prophetic. Theo went home via the florist's.

'Celebrating our news from yesterday?' Madison asked, after kissing him thank you for the two dozen pink roses.

'No. Celebrating our news from today.'

She tipped her head slightly to one side. 'What news?'

He picked her up and whirled her round. 'I got the job. As from Monday, I'm officially the senior consultant.'

'Theo, that's wonderful!'

'So I'm taking you out to dinner tonight to celebrate.' He smiled. 'I'm doing drinks and a curry for the team on Friday—which obviously includes you, *agapi mou*—but tonight I want to celebrate just with my wife-to-be.' He stroked her abdomen. 'And our daughter.' And then as he felt a flutter against his fingertips, he had to sit down. 'Maddie. She just kicked me.'

'You felt it, too? I felt a fluttering last week, as if someone was blowing bubbles inside me, but I thought it was my imagination.'

'No. And I didn't think you could feel a baby kick this early. But she definitely responded.' He pressed his face against Madison's abdomen. 'I love you,' he whispered. *'S'agapi, kardoula mou.'*

'If she can twist you round her little finger at this stage, heaven help you when she's a teenager. All she'll have to do is bat her eyes at you and say, "I love you, Daddy," and you'll be putty in her hands,' Madison said, laughing.

'I will not. I'll be a stern Greek father.'

'Sure you will.' Madison chuckled. 'You'll probably terrify her boyfriends. But you'll be a complete pushover where our baby's concerned. And don't deny it—Sophie's told me what kind of uncle you are.'

His eyes widened. 'You talk to Sophie?'

'She emails me. So does Meli—who's going to come over when I'm on maternity leave and teach me to cook.'

'You, learn to cook? Now, this,' he said with a grin, 'I have to see.'

'You just wait,' she said primly, but her eyes were sparkling.

Over dinner, Madison said thoughtfully, 'They say things come in threes—I wonder what the third one will be?'

'Baby, job… How about getting married?' he suggested. Madison had so far refused to set a date for the wedding and it was driving him crackers.

'Not until the baby's here,' she said firmly.

He knew better than to start a pointless battle. 'OK. How about a new house to go with the new job and the new baby?'

She blinked. 'House?'

'I'm settled in London now, and if you want to stay here too then it makes sense for us to buy a place rather than rent. And this place isn't really going to be big enough for a growing family.'

'Well, I've got some savings,' she said.

'No need. My family's wealthy, *kardoula mou*. Dad gave us all a fairly big chunk of money when we graduated—well, Stefanos obviously hasn't got his yet, but he will do. I spent mine on a house. I sold it last year, and made quite a profit. I have enough for a substantial deposit. So let's go house-hunting.'

'Seriously?'

'Seriously,' he confirmed. 'I can provide for you, Maddie.'

She folded her arms. 'Spare me the macho-man bit, Theo. This is the twenty-first century. I don't expect you to provide for me—but I do expect a real marriage. An equal partnership. So we'll do this together or we won't do it at all.'

'You know, we're definitely going to have to have another baby,' Theo said. 'A son. To even the balance in our house.'

Madison laughed. 'Yes, dear.'

Luck was on their side—not only did they find the perfect house in the first week of looking but there was no chain because the previous owners had sold it to a developer in a part-exchange deal. A month later, and the house was theirs. Theo organised decorators— '*Agapi mou*, the paint fumes won't be good for the baby, and anyway painting walls will give you backache,' he informed Madison when she protested.

'This is going to be the best Christmas ever,' Madison said in satisfaction when they moved in. 'My parents are coming to stay, your family are flying over from Greece—and maybe your grandparents might join us.' Although Theo had made his peace with them when he'd moved to England, she'd noticed that they were still reserved with him. Though his grandmother had seemed to thaw a little when they'd told her they were expecting a little girl.

Christmas was as big and noisy as Madison had planned. Their families liked each other; there were no tensions about whose traditions were being used because, as Madison herself put it, it was a new house and a new joint family and this was their first Christmas together. The entire time seemed to be filled with laughter and planning a spring wedding and a christening.

When Madison slipped quietly into the kitchen to put the kettle on, Eleni followed her. 'I just wanted to say thank you, Madison,' she said quietly. 'Because of you, my boy doesn't have shadows in his eyes any more.' She smiled wryly. 'I say "my boy"—I know he's only borrowed, but I love him like my own. And I can't wait for my third grandchild to arrive.'

'Eleni, you *are* my mother,' Theo said softly.

'Theo? Where did you come from?'

'Just making sure Maddie isn't overdoing things.' He took her hands. 'Why do you think I'm only borrowed, *kardoula mou*?'

Eleni shrugged. 'You stopped calling me *Mamá* after we told you about your mother.'

'I was fifteen, at a difficult age, and I had a lot to get my head round—but, yes, you're right, I've avoided using the word,' Theo admitted. 'And I'm sorry. It's not because I don't love you, because I do. You've always been there for me. And

I've always thought of you as mine.' He smiled at her. '*S'agapo, Mamá.*'

Eleni's eyes filled with tears. '*S'agapo, yios mou.* I love you, too, my son.'

Madison, seeing the expressions on their faces, knew that the final brick wall was down. Everything was going to be fine.

Three weeks later, Madison was pottering around the house. She'd woken in the night with a slight stomachache, but had simply turned over and gone back to sleep, thinking she'd eaten something that had disagreed with her slightly.

But in the middle of the afternoon it suddenly hit her. She'd been having stomachache on and off all day. A stomachache that wasn't a stomachache: she was having contractions.

'I can't be,' she said out loud. 'It's too early.' Three weeks too early.

Maybe it was Braxton-Hicks', the 'practice' contractions that fooled many a first-time mum-to-be into calling the midwife.

But she knew it had been going on too long.

She thought about ringing Theo—but, then again, what was the point in making him come home from work, only to go straight back to the ward? Instead, she called a taxi and carried her own bag up to the ward.

'Maddie! Lovely to see you.' Iris greeted her with a hug. 'Are you meeting Theo from work? He's in clinic at the moment.'

'I know.' And the contractions were still reasonably far apart. It was way too early to book herself in. 'Mind if I wait in his office?' she asked.

'Sure. Do you want one of us to get you a drink?'

Maddie laughed. 'I'm eight and a bit months pregnant, not ill. But thanks for the offer.'

She amused herself catching up with journals until Theo walked through the door.

'Hello—I didn't expect to see you here.' He greeted her with a kiss. 'Bored at home, are you?'

'Something like that,' Madison said.

Then he caught sight of her hospital bag. 'Is that what I think it is?' At her nod, he raked a hand through his hair. 'You impossible woman—why didn't you call me?'

'There was no point when you're here anyway—it was quicker for me to come here than to wait for you to get all the way home and bring me all the way back here,' she explained.

'When did you start having contractions?'

'In the middle of the night. Except I thought it was indigestion.'

'And you an obstetrician. Tut-tut.' He was clearly trying to be smiley and jokey, but Madison caught a glimpse of fear in his eyes.

She needed to distract him.

She glanced up at the clock. 'The last one was ten minutes ago and it's just starting again now. So you might want to come and book me in.'

He went pale. 'Oh, lord. I think I've just forgotten everything I know about babies.'

She squeezed his hand. 'You're not delivering this baby, Theo. The midwifery team is.'

'The midwifery team is what?' Iris asked from the doorway.

'Um, attending to me. Today.'

'I thought you were having a February baby?'

'This one has a mind of her own. She's decided that she wants to be a new year baby.'

'As of now,' Theo said, 'I'm unavailable. Iris, I'll go and get a wheelchair—'

'You'll do nothing of the kind,' Madison interrupted. 'You know as well as I do that it's good for women in labour to walk about and let gravity do its stuff.'

'Maddie, I can't even think straight,' he admitted.

Iris came over and patted his shoulder. 'It's nice to see that when it comes to his own baby, our senior consultant is just like any other anxious dad-to-be. Come on. Let's get you booked in.'

'Theo, it's going to be all right,' Madison said softly when Iris had left Theo's office. 'I know there's a part of you that's worrying, but it's going to be just fine.'

Eight hours later, Theo was cradling his daughter in his arms. 'I've never seen anyone so beautiful in my entire life. With the exception perhaps of her mother.'

Madison laughed. 'I'm sweaty and smelly and I'm desperate for a hair-wash.'

'You're still beautiful, *agapi mou*,' he told her sincerely. 'And so is our baby.'

He'd driven Madison crazy over the last few months, refusing to discuss names and saying that they'd know her name when they saw her. 'She needs to be called something other than "Baby Petrakis",' Madison said. 'So I was wondering…now she's here, would you like to call her after your mother?'

Theo shook his head. 'Maybe as a middle name. And we'd also need your mother's and Eleni's names as middle names, too. No. I think she needs her own name.'

She had a feeling that he had something in mind. 'Which is?' she asked softly.

'Helen. Not as in Helen of Troy—Helen, from its original root of *helios*, meaning "sun". Because you've brought so much sunshine into my life, Maddie. And our daughter's going to be so much a part of that.'

She swallowed hard. 'Theo, that's beautiful. I think I'm going to cry.'

'That's hormones, *kardoula mou*,' he said with a smile.

'My two best girls. The light of my life. It doesn't get any better than this, Maddie.' He leaned over to kiss her. 'And you know what? It's going to be like this for the rest of our days.'